HUNGRY FOR HER BEAR

HUNGRY FUR LOVE
BOOK 2

C.D. GORRI

DEDICATION

To my Beta & ARC Teams for all you do. No release would be the same without you.

To my good friends Patricia & Julia who constantly cheer me on and have made this writing journey a phenomenal one.

& To all the fans and readers who've stuck with me on this crazy ride through indie publishing. You amaze me and have my gratitude.

del mare alla stella,

C.D. Gorri

HUNGRY FOR HER BEAR
HUNGRY FUR LOVE 2 COPYRIGHT

By C.D. Gorri
Edited by BookNookNuts
Copyright © 2022, 2025

Hungry For Her Bear © 2022, 2025 C.D. Gorri

HUNGRY FUR LOVE
THE SERIES

Welcome to Castor's Corner—where the witches are curvy, the magic is unpredictable, and the fated mates come with fur, fangs, and deliciously dirty minds.

The witch trifecta of Castor's Corner is made up of three over-thirty besties who might be a magical mess, but they've got hearts of gold and zero time for nonsense—unless it comes in the form of a smoldering supernatural male.

As the guardians of their quirky, chaos-prone town, these witches are supposed to keep things under control.

Then the barrier goes down, and all magical hell breaks loose.

Now the town's crawling with trouble: ghouls in

the cemetery, talking pets with attitude, ghostly family drama, and worst of all—gorgeous shifters who might just be their fated mates.

These sexy strangers are growly, protective, and utterly devoted. And they're not backing off, no matter how messy things get.

If you love:

✔ Fated mates who can't resist a curvy witch

✔ Magical mischief and hilarious spell fails

✔ Steamy slow burns with a side of claws and cuddles

✔ Found family, fierce friendship, and paranormal chaos

Then buckle up, buttercup. The Hungry Fur Love series is here to cast a spell on your heart—and maybe your underwear.

Dive into this sizzling romcom series full of heart, heat, and happily-ever-afters with bite today!

HUNGRY FOR HER BEAR

A CURVY WITCH **Meets Baker Bear Shifter Fated Mates Romance**

A haunted salon, a broody Bear Shifter, and one very bad hair day. Can magic fix this mess?

Will I let a swoony Bear Shifter help me face my past, fix my magic, and save Castor's Corner—again?

Ugh. Probably. But I don't have to like it.

See, Castor's Corner is special. Magical. And a total pain in my perfectly-toned Witchy behind.

Some people think I'm just a small-town stylist with a flair for facials and fabulous blowouts.

Okay, yes—I'm a goddess with a curling iron, and yes, beauty does matter. But my true gift? Helping people feel like the best version of themselves, inside and out. Magic through makeovers, baby.

Still, I'm more than just a killer cut and color. I'm one-third of the Trifecta protecting our supernatural town. And lately? Things have been hectic.

Ever since we accidentally let down the barrier, we've had a parade of paranormal drama: spooky new neighbors, a mystery Ghost in the salon, my new grumpy familiar who hates my guts, and Ryan— the seven-foot-tall, croissant-baking, brown-eyed Bear Shifter who makes me feel all kinds of things I do not have time for.

Did I mention he's the only one who can help me channel my out-of-whack powers and save my maybe-grandpa from Purgatory?

Now there's a blood moon rising just in time for the town's Halloween Bash, and chaos is coming for us in a glittery, cursed, candy-coated storm.

So yeah. My BFFs and I have one job.

Protect the town. Again.

Easy. If I can keep my hands off the Bear.

PROLOGUE-DONNY

THE SUN WAS SHINING when I left for work this morning, as it always seemed to on crisp Autumn mornings in Castor's Corner.

Like the Goddess herself was mood-lighting the whole damn town.

Maybe She was trying to butter me up. If so, She was doing a good job of it.

The day passed by in a whoosh of appointments and fashion fiascos, and now, we'd just finished charging our wards, protecting the town.

Even so, I could still feel it as I stood beneath the pale moonlight.

There's just something about fall that makes everything feel a little more enchanted.

The air gets that bitey edge, your sweaters start looking cuter, and the leaves go full drama queen.

And let me tell you, nobody does foliage like South Jersey.

Our trees go full-on peacock every October—flashing colors like they're competing in a magical Miss America pageant.

The pines keep it classy, of course, but the maples? The oaks?

Those show-offs burst into flaming oranges and reds like they're about to storm a runway.

There are even some purples, the kind that make you feel like you fell into a bottle of cabernet and never looked back.

Even the birches get their shimmer on.

It was no coincidence that my birthday landed right smack in the middle of fall.

October 18th, baby.

A Libra to my glittery little core.

And yes, I was feeling every one of my *mature, magical* years that morning.

Not that I'd tell you my exact age, so don't even ask.

Witches live long lives, okay?

Some of us just do it while still looking like cover models for *Wands & Wine Weekly*.

But even though I looked fluffy and fabulous—*and I did, thank you very much*—my age was a bit of a sore subject.

Probably because I'd yet to find someone to share my present *or* my future with.

Someone who could handle all *this*—the curves, the sass, the moonlit rituals, and, oh yeah, the chaotic magical energy that sometimes sparks out of my fingers like I'm cosplaying a lightning bug on meth.

So yeah. The past?

Not really my favorite topic.

It was full of failed almost-romances, regrettable eyebrow shapes, and an unfortunate incident with a talking vibrator and a cursed drawer that I still refuse to discuss.

Let's just say—*I stay busy*.

I run my salon, *Hair Now, Gone Tomorrow,* I co-guard the magical wardings of this entire town with my besties-slash-soul sisters, and when things get really dire, I turn to my trusty drawer of battery-operated back-up plans.

You know the kind.

The kind you do *not* use in a group setting—unless you're in a very different kind of Coven.

Castor's Corner hadn't exactly been overflowing with viable man meat lately.

At least, not until *they* showed up.

The trio of supernatural hotties that had blown into town like the world's sexiest natural disaster.

My powers always got twitchy around newcomers, but this time?

Full-on tingle fest.

Every time I caught a glimpse of the grumpy Bear Shifter working at the firehouse-slash-bakery, my magic decided to perform an internal jazz hands routine.

Which was concerning.

Especially because Ryan McLeod looked like he could break me in half and then bake me a pie to apologize.

And that? That was a problem.

But right now I have different concerns.

Mainly my besties who were whispering about me with freaking blow horns or so it seemed.

"So, what are we doing for her birthday this year?" Bella asked Evie in the worst attempt at a stage whisper I'd ever heard.

I didn't bother to hide my groan.

Not this shit again.

It was no secret I hated birthdays. Mine especially.

Nothing like being reminded that your existence was a side note in your own parents' epic love story.

A plot twist they barely remembered, let alone celebrated.

Yeah, I had issues. But who didn't?

The thing was, I wasn't pouting about it anymore.

Not since learning Evie and Bella weren't just my best friends—they were my blood.

Cousins.

Real family.

The kind that didn't forget your birthday.

Even when you really, really wished they would.

"Ladies," I drawled, narrowing my eyes at the two conspirators. "I'm still here. I have ears. Magical, highly sensitive, stunningly symmetrical ears."

Evie ignored me, as usual, giving Bella a wide-eyed shrug like I hadn't just threatened her with bodily glittering. Which was fair.

I'd already doused them in pink glitter rain once this week, and honestly, it did nothing to deter them.

If anything, they looked sparkly and smug.

It was the night of our monthly boundary ceremony.

You know—the thing that kept clueless humans from wandering into our little supernatural haven.

We were standing around a roaring bonfire, the flames dancing higher than usual, crackling with layered spells and protective intent.

All very serious. Very mystical. Very important.

And yet there they were—giggling and plotting like my entire disdain for birthday parties wasn't a matter of public record.

I crossed my arms over my chest, casting a narrowed glance toward the firehouse where smoke curled into the night sky and the unmistakable scent of grilled meat wafted through the cool air.

Of course.

The three new Shifter additions to our town were out there flipping burgers and searing steaks like they weren't sex on legs with sharp teeth and mysterious pasts.

I could practically feel the hormonal haze wafting off Evie and Bella from here.

Evie's fated mate, Jaxson, had already claimed her.

The Wolfy Sheriff had broody eyes and a body that did deeply sinful things to denim—not that I noticed. He wasn't mine, after all.

But I did approve of how he treated Evie. And I was happy for them.

Mostly.

Bella was dancing around her own animalistic tension with one of the other two Shifters, and I'd bet my limited-edition Jimmy Choos that this whole freaking *birthday party* idea was cooked up as an excuse to gather under the pretensc of cake and awkward presents.

The heifers.

"AHH!"

"Donny!"

The glitter storm hit them mid-conspiracy, raining golden flecks over their heads and shoulders.

They squealed, of course.

But it was practically a tradition at this point in our lives.

They plot. I bomb. Period.

"Oops," I said, smirking. "My wand sneezed."

They glared at me, but I was already flicking my wrist and redressing myself in something that made me feel like me—*Lafayette 148 New York cashmere, wide-leg silk and linen-blend pants.*

Earthy taupe tones—perfect for my skin color and my dark hair.

Elegant without trying too hard.

Magical but minimal.

We weren't typical Witches, not in Castor's Corner.

Evie had that effortless retro glam thing going on —like a 1960s siren met a horror movie hostess and they decided to run for mayor.

Bella was a garden nymph come to life. Bows, florals, the occasional pastel tulle.

And me? I was couture curves, top to toe. If it had structure and softness, I'd wear it.

And if it didn't come in my size? I'd make it.

Being curvy in a supernatural world came with its challenges.

Shifters could eat three times their weight and still look like a damn Marvel superhero.

But our Trifecta? We were soft, strong, and undeniably magical.

My magic hummed in my veins as I looked around the fire-lit circle.

It wasn't just vanity.

This was about presence.

Power.

Claiming our space in a world that often tried to squeeze us into smaller boxes—*both literal and metaphorical.*

I used magic to tailor designer pieces not just for

me, but for others in the town who deserved to see themselves in velvet, in silk, in sequins.

We weren't invisible.

We were divine.

"Still trying to throw me a party?" I asked them, softer now.

Bella grinned, unrepentant. "What gave it away?"

"The utter lack of subtlety," I said. "And the glitter in your hair."

Evie stepped beside me, giving my hand a squeeze.

"You don't have to celebrate if you don't want to. But, well, *we* want to celebrate *you*."

I didn't answer right away.

The truth was—*I wanted to believe them.*

I wanted to lean into it, into the possibility that maybe birthdays didn't have to suck.

That, maybe, being seen, being loved, was something I could allow without bracing for disappointment.

"I'll think about it," I said finally.

Which was basically a yes in Donny-speak.

The girls knew it too.

Bella bounced on her heels, and Evie's eyes shimmered in the firelight.

Ugh. Emotions. Gross.

"Now, if you'll excuse me," I huffed, executing a full-bodied twirl like the dramatic queen I am. "I have a hot date with a medium-rare steak and a sinfully spicy book series Stanley told me not to read in public."

"Nuh uh, Donny dear," Bella said, snapping her fingers and hooking her arm through mine like a determined Disney villain sidekick. "You're eating with us tonight."

"Wait—*why?* Did I lose a bet? Am I being punished for something I said in a past life?"

"Because we're family, you glorious, sparkly beyotch," Bella hissed like a trashy soap opera villain and somehow made it sound like a love confession.

It was honestly pitiful how much I adored her.

"She's right," Evie chimed in, always the cool mom of our trio. "We're family. We're hungry. And let's face it, none of us knows how to portion control. So whaddya say? Come, break bread—or, you know, *meat*—with us?"

I squinted suspiciously. "Where?"

"Firehouse. The boys are grilling," Evie answered, eyes gleaming like she just got away with shoplifting from a Sephora.

They both burst out laughing like the maniacal Witches they are.

And for once?

So did I.

Because even though I had spicy books, leftover steak, and a perfectly fluff-folded blanket waiting for me at home, there was something even better about dinner with the people who made my life feel like magic.

Even if they wcrc bossy, nosy, and constantly trying to fatten me up for some future supernatural bake-off.

Family, right?

Dangerous.

But worth it.

CHAPTER ONE-DONNY

DID I forget to introduce myself before?

My name is Donatella Andrews. AKA Donny.

Trifecta Witch. Stylist. And entrepreneur.

I own my own salon here in Castor's Corner, and I had several interests, but *beauty* was my number one.

See, life wasn't always kind to the curvy girls of the world, but that just made me dig my perfectly manicured heels in harder.

I'd made it my personal mission to be a force for women—*especially the ones society didn't always celebrate.*

We came in all shapes, sizes, and supernatural species here in Castor's Corner, and I considered it my sacred Witchy duty (and aesthetic responsibility) to help every last one of them feel like the magic they were born to be.

That meant everything from waxing Shifters who went furry more often than full moon legends care to admit, to formulating wart-banishing creams for the Troll sisters who liked their skin smooth and shimmer-free for their monthly mahjong nights—*they're surprisingly competitive, and very into tea tree oil and cucumber facials.*

My salon wasn't just a place to get your brows snatched or your aura cleansed—it was a *sanctuary.*

A safe space.

A spell-charged, vanilla-citrus-scented temple to self-love.

As for me, Evie, and Bella?

Well, our problem wasn't razor burn or horn polish.

It was our hips.

Specifically, the fact that they didn't lie—and neither did our thighs, bellies, or butts.

Sigh.

You see, supernaturals typically burn calories like toddlers on espresso, but for some reason, the magical Trifecta of Castor's Corner didn't get that particular blessing.

While most supes could wolf down five pizzas

and still fit into enchanted body-con rune-suits, the three of us actually had to watch what we ate.

Spoiler: we didn't.

And honestly?

Fuck society's view of what we looked like.

I wasn't here for anyone's approval. I was here to elevate what we already had—and in my not-so-humble opinion, what we had was a lot.

We were juicy.

Voluptuous.

Powerful.

Dangerous in the best way.

Sure, we all dealt with one form of social anxiety or another. Evie hid hers behind Mayor-level sass and vintage cardigans.

Bella turned hers into sparkly optimism and edible glitter.

And me? I wore mine under designer threads, six layers of self-confidence, and enough hair serum to smooth a Yeti.

But deep down, we felt it.

That quiet hum of not-enoughness that followed girls like us since the cradle.

And you know what?

We were so done with that.

Because all I knew—for a chubby magical trio of BFFs from South Jersey?

We were hot as fuck.

Hotter than hellfire in stilettos.

Stronger than the enchanted arches on our town square.

And ready to hex the hell out of anyone who said otherwise.

So yeah. Life hadn't always been kind.

But we were.

To each other.

And to ourselves.

And that? That was the kind of magic this world desperately needed.

Seriously.

So what if we had curves for days? We also had humor, brains, sass, and cheekbones that could cut glass (when properly contoured). Not to mention enough magical juice to light up every crystal in a five-mile radius.

Even better? Bella, Evie, and I weren't just besties anymore.

Turns out we were cousins, too.

Family by blood and bond.

Together, we made up one seriously powerful

Witch Trifecta, reinforcing the magical perimeter of Castor's Corner every month like clockwork since puberty.

Warding off humans, bad vibes, and the occasional cryptid with boundary issues.

Easy peasy.

Most of the time.

And we always did our duty—well, sorta.

I mean, it wasn't always easy being a Trifecta Witch.

For example, there was that time Bella was late to our bonfire, and the wards went kaput for exactly forty-seven seconds, and a banshee wandered into town and scared the piss out of poor Old Man Clive at the grocery store.

But hey, it was once.

One time.

And technically Clive had it coming—he still uses coupons from 1997 and hits on the entire staff of every store in town.

Even the mail office—and I'm pretty sure he's related to the postmaster.

And most recently, of course, was Evie's recent mishap. Her tardiness was the reason we now had three maddening males in our midst.

Sure, she happened to find her fated mate among

them. And good for her. But now I had to deal with seeing *him* on a regular basis.

Do not go there, Donny, I warned myself.

For me, being single wasn't an accident. It was a choice.

Tell yourself that.

Sometimes I really hated my inner voice.

Anyway, the point is we always tried to be extra careful.

But shit, *as they say,* happens.

They talk a whole lot, don't they?

Anyway, there we were, wrapping up another uneventful strengthening of the town's wards bonfire night.

Easy as pie.

Nothing doing.

But honestly? Something felt off.

Maybe it was the end-of-summer air curling in with that bone-deep warning that things were about to change.

Or maybe it was just my usual low-key birthday dread starting early.

I hated birthdays.

Always had.

Too much pressure, not enough cake.

And don't even get me started on the years my parents forgot entirely.

Nothing says childhood trauma like a half-eaten Entenmann's and a card addressed to the cat.

No, I wasn't in the mood for celebration.

And these two knew that.

"We just wanna celebrate you," Bella wailed, all blonde curls and drama, her arms flailing like a caffeinated fairy godmother as she summoned a massive fluffy pink towel from thin air.

A matching blue one landed on Evie, who gave her a look like *really*, and started drying off her boobs with the kind of nonchalance only a Mayor-slash-Witch could pull off.

I crossed my arms and tried not to laugh.

I'd soaked them with a little glitter rain for bringing up my birthday again.

Was it petty? Maybe.

Was it hilarious? Absolutely.

So yeah, I did it again. Drenching the towels this time, too.

"Donny!" they both screeched at me, as if I hadn't been pulling this exact stunt for the past decade.

"Love you," I sing-songed, flicking my wrist to change into one of my favorite Lafayette 148 cashmere sweaters and wide-leg silk-linen pants.

Designer duds and magic? A match made in retail therapy heaven.

Typical Witches couldn't cast for personal gain. Nope. That was a big *no-no* in the magical world.

But we weren't the average trio of Witches.

We were curvy, magical, and fabulous—*and we owned it*.

Always had.

Always would.

Castor's Corner might've been our hometown, but we brought the sparkle, sass, and snark to every single bonfire, bake sale, and battle with ancient evil.

Evie rocked her whole retro glam aesthetic like a pin-up librarian who could hex you into a frog and still make you blush.

Bella was pure pastel chaos in floral prints with dimples of doom.

And me? I liked clean lines, bold colors, and labels that didn't think plus size meant potato sack chic.

And for the record?

I had never been zapped by the Goddess for magicking a Chanel blazer into a size twenty-two.

So I took that as cosmic approval.

After we all changed into dry clothes and removed the glitter bomb residue from our skin, we linked arms like the magical coven of badasses we were and headed toward the Castor's Corner Firehouse.

And just like I knew they would be, there *they* were.

The Shifters.

Three larger-than-life, ridiculously handsome, and unfairly built supernatural snacks grilling half a cow over a spit like it was the Stone Age.

But at least they made it hot.

Literally hot—*there were flames involved.*

And biceps. So many biceps.

Some locals were there too, mingling, munching, and making nice.

Apparently, the big boys had been making themselves right at home.

And the worst part? The town liked them.

Great.

Jaxson Reid was a given.

He was Evie's fated mate, after all.

Town Sheriff, swoony mate, and sweet on her in a way that made me both sigh and roll my eyes.

He spotted her the second we walked up and practically ran over like a golden retriever in a flannel shirt.

He swept her up into one of those bone-melting

embraces that made everyone around them go *awww* and me go *gag*.

Okay, fine, I was a little jealous. Shut up.

Still, I couldn't blame her. If someone looked at me the way Jaxson looked at Evie, I'd probably cry and drop my panties at the same time.

Which brought me to the other two Shifters standing there looking way too good for it to be legal.

Conrad Boman. Python Shifter. Tall, pale, coiled energy in a fireproof shirt, and one hundred percent obsessed with Bella.

Dude's eyes followed her like he was waiting for her to drop her lip gloss so he could propose.

Bella, being Bella, hadn't noticed. Or maybe she had and was pretending not to. Hard to tell with that one.

But I sure did. And Conrad Boman was definitely into the curvy little Witch.

And then there was Ryan McLeod.

Grizzly Bear Shifter.

Massive.

Broody.

Delicious.

Built like a tree trunk with arms thick enough to bench press a school bus.

He didn't look at anyone the way Jaxson looked at Evie. He didn't follow Bella with his gaze like Conrad did.

Nope.

But he looked at me.

Sometimes.

From under his lashes.

When he thought I wasn't paying attention.

Spoiler alert: I always paid attention.

Problem was, I didn't know what to do with it. My heart hadn't exactly been open for business lately.

Hell, I wasn't even sure the power was on inside.

Still, Ryan McLeod made it flicker.

He made something stir deep inside of me.

And that was terrifying. Alarming. Disturbing. And definitely not allowed.

So I crossed my arms, adjusted my hair, and pretended not to care.

Classic Donatella defense.

But inside?

Inside, I was gulping.

Because when a Bear like that looks at a Witch like me, all bets are off.

And I wasn't sure I was ready to find out what happened when he finally made a move.

But I had a feeling it was coming.

And when it did?

Well.

Gaia help me.

I just hoped I didn't melt faster than the marsh-mallows toasting over that fire.

CHAPTER THREE-RYAN

THERE SHE IS. Donatella Andrews.

The Witch of my dreams.

Literal dreams, okay?

Not some kind of poetic metaphor.

Ever since the damn truck broke down and stranded me, Jaxson, and Conrad in Castor's Corner, my Bear has been restless as hell.

Pacing, snarling, demanding—*hers*. Mostly just hers.

Like he's just waiting for her to look our way and say the word.

I thought the town was cursed at first.

I mean, the mayor's a Witch, the bakery talks to itself (don't ask), and someone keeps hexing the firehouse bathroom so every time you walk into the damn stall, it plays *Back That Azz Up*.

But the real madness?

It's her.

Donny.

She's all fire and glitter and that big city-meets-small town kind of fabulous that makes my brain short-circuit every time she struts by in some designer getup I can't even pronounce.

Her hair always looks like she just stepped out of a shampoo commercial.

Her laugh is too loud for any one woman to own.

And her curves? Her fucking curves.

Gaia help me.

My Bear wants to worship every inch of her like she's a damn altar.

She doesn't even look at me.

Correction—she looks at me like I'm one of those novelty air fresheners that smells like beef jerky.

Intriguing.

Confusing.

Possibly offensive.

Meanwhile, I'm working double time—literally.

Fighting fires during the day, baking croissants, rolls, baguettes, and even pies at *The Tasty Tart* at night.

with a voice like sugar and a temper like a spring-loaded trap.

Bella smiles like sunshine—but if you ever make her cry, she'll probably turn you into a muffin.

But Bella isn't mine.

Neither is Evie.

They're both powerful, sexy, wonderful Witches—but the Fates didn't tie me to either of them.

No.

They gave me Donatella.

Donny Freaking Andrews.

And if the Fates had a sense of humor, they were pissing themselves laughing right now.

Because I'm not exactly what Donny would call *her type*.

I mean, unless *her type* included large, broody Bear Shifters who baked in their spare time, had zero fashion sense, and looked like they could bench press a Buick—*which, for the record, I could.*

But none of that seemed to matter to her. Because when she looked at me—*which wasn't nearly often enough*—it was with that *you've got flour on your shirt and also your face* kind of expression.

Meanwhile, I'm over here losing my damn mind because her laugh makes my chest feel like it's catching fire and her curves?

Let's just say my Bear gets *hungry*.

See, I'm the kind of guy who once I've made up my mind about something, I don't stop.

I don't change it.

I don't lose focus.

And Donny?

She might be avoiding me, ignoring me, pretending I'm just some temporary help with a whisk and a hero complex.

But if she ever gives me the time of day?

She's gonna find out exactly what it means to mess with a Bear's affections.

I'll ruin her lipstick, worship her thighs, whisper filthy things in her ear while she's cutting hair or re-organizing the fashion world just to make her squirm.

I'll mark her, claim her, and cherish her until she realizes the Goddess herself made her for me.

But until then?

I'll wait.

I'll watch.

I'll burn quietly every time she walks into a room and acts like her presence isn't wrecking my entire ecosystem.

Because looking at her and not being able to touch her?

It's the sweetest kind of hell I can imagine.

I should leave.

I should pack up and get the hell out of Dodge—er, Castor's Corner.

But I won't. I can't.

All because I know.

Deep in my bones, beneath the aching need and the slow simmering want, I know the truth.

She's mine.

And I'm not going anywhere.

Just then, Donny bends over to inspect something on the far end of the table, her plump ass outlined in the pants she has on, and I squeeze the tongs in my hand so tightly they snap.

Yep, I am just that cool.

Fuck me sideways.

I swear the Goddess herself is laughing at me this time.

CHAPTER FOUR-DONNY

I WATCHED Jaxson and Evie for a whole minute before I turned and started loading my plate with some calorie-filled love.

I wasn't jealous.

Not exactly.

Okay, so I envied them.

Not for long, mind you—*just a fleeting moment.*

Just long enough to see Jaxson scoop up my mayoral cousin Evie like she was the last donut on earth and smother her with one of those made-for-cable movie kisses.

The kind where the world fades out, the music swells, and somewhere in the background a raccoon sheds a single tear because true love is real.

And damn it, I was happy for her.

My jealousy slipped away like butter on a hot skillet, because if anyone deserved a *happily ever after*, it was Evie.

Especially after all the magical chaos, political nonsense, and bad date stories she'd had to endure as mayor and mateless Witch of Castor's Corner.

Plate filled, I was about to find myself a quiet corner to eat when I was stopped in my tracks.

"Oooh, Donny! Check out this bread," Bella gasped, pulling me back to the present like a high-pitched fairy godmother with poor impulse control.

I turned and followed her gaze to the table, where a holy offering of food awaited.

Baguettes.

Real ones.

Not the fake, keto-friendly, cardboard bread I've been trying out.

These were the real thing, sitting there like a treasure trove in all their gluten-glory.

Crisp crusts, golden brown, practically singing in French.

I zeroed in on one that had the right amount of air pockets and density inside—bready perfection.

I was pretty sure the last time I saw carbs that beautiful I had proposed.

"Where'd they get it?" I asked, already mentally composing a love sonnet to gluten.

"Me," came the rumble from behind me.

And just like that, my inner peace shattered.

I felt him before I saw him.

The heat rolling off that massive body, like he was my own personal furnace—*if said furnace smelled like cinnamon, warm cedar, and dirty promises.*

Ryan McLeod.

The Grizzly Bear Shifter with forearms the size of Christmas hams, and a voice that did things to my reproductive organs that I didn't have the time, energy, or emotional bandwidth to examine.

And let me tell you, that voice? It was pure slow-drip seduction.

Like dark-roasted coffee poured straight into your soul and stirred with a stick of sin.

I didn't even glance over my shoulder.

Instead, I channeled my inner ice queen, rolled my eyes, and sauntered to the far end of the table in my fabulously impractical high-heeled boots.

I could feel him watching me, but I didn't look back.

No way was I about to make bedroom eyes at the man who had single-handedly turned my brain into fondue the second he showed up in town.

Because I was not a one-night-stand kind of girl.

I was a whole damn seven-course-meal with candlelight and custom playlist kind of woman.

And I did not have time for hot, broody distractions with thighs that could crack watermelons.

And also?

My heart had the structural integrity of a meringue.

So no. No, no, nope.

"Fucking hell, this is gonna suck," I muttered under my breath, just as a devious little voice purred in my ear.

"So, whatcha think of these guys? Looks like they're fitting in around here."

"Fucking fuckety fuck, Bella!" I shrieked, flailing so hard I dropped my plate like a doomed frisbee and slapped a hand over my chest. "You scared the fucking fuck outta me!"

The entire firehouse went silent.

Every eyeball turned.

Bella's jaw hit the floor.

Evie winced like someone had just stepped on her crystals.

And me? I realized I'd just racked up a record-breaking number of f-bombs in one sentence.

Even for me.

Which, frankly, was impressive.

"Uh-oh," Evie whispered.

Too late.

The Goddess was listening.

A streak of magic—*bright, furious, and bubble-gum pink*—shot down from the heavens like a cosmic slap on the ass.

And I mean that literally.

"EEEEEEK! I'M ON FIRE!" I yowled, grabbing my butt and doing an involuntary twerk of terror. "SOMEONE CALL 9-1-FREAKING-1!"

But of course, the literal fire station was already here, and in the most humiliating twist of fate, it was Ryan Freaking McLeod who stepped in with the garden hose.

Not the fancy magical rain spell I'd spent years perfecting.

Not a cooling potion.

No. A basic ass hose.

Whoosh—*I got doused like a cat in a bathtub.*

Water splashed into my eyes, down my cleavage, and straight through my linen blouse.

I now resembled a drowned Witch rat in designer pants and ruined hair.

Excellent.

"You alright?" he asked, eyes full of genuine

concern, which was just the cherry on top of my humiliation sundae.

Was I alright?

I was drenched, humiliated, and somehow still turned on by the seven-foot-tall Bear with a bakery apron and a rescue complex.

I did what any self-respecting Witch would do.

I straightened my spine, flipped my soaking wet curls over my shoulder with as much dignity as I could muster, spit out the water that had sloshed into my mouth, and hit him square in the chest with it.

Then I turned on my soggy heel and left.

Behind me, Bella was laughing so hard she snorted.

Evie clapped a hand over her mouth.

Ryan, well, the bastard just smiled.

Smiled.

Even though he had a wet spot right where I hit him.

Jerk.

I hated him.

I also maybe, possibly, wanted to climb him like a sexy, boulder-sized jungle gym and never come down.

FML.

CHAPTER FIVE-RYAN

There's pining, and then there's me—*sitting on a half-deflated couch cushion, staring blankly at a cold cup of coffee, wondering what the fucking hell is wrong with me.*

It's not like I haven't been around women before.

I've had flings.

I've had things.

Hell, I've had one-night stands that stretched into three-day weekends.

But Donatella Andrews?

She's not *a* thing.

She's *the* thing.

My Bear knows it.

Has known it since the second we stepped foot in this magical madhouse of a town.

She's it.

Our mate.

Our future.

The problem?

She won't give me the damned time of day.

"I take it this is your *pining in silence* phase?"

Jaxson's voice cut through my self-loathing like a buzz saw through kindling.

I looked up to find the smug bastard leaning against the doorjamb like some Abercrombie ad for municipal authority.

New Sheriff badge gleaming, aviators tucked into his front pocket, and that annoying alpha male smirk plastered across his face.

"What are you doing here?" I grumbled. "Didn't you move out with your mate into that love shack of yours?"

"Sure did," he said, strolling in like he owned the place. "But I left my flannel hoodie here and came back for it. Then I saw you staring into space like a rejected country song and figured I'd check in."

"Thanks, but I don't need a therapist in tight jeans. Cute. You thinking about joining a boy band next?"

"Come on, Ry," Jaxson flopped into the chair across from me, lacing his hands behind his head. "I've been where you are. Evie had me doing backflips before she even admitted we were mates. It sucks. I get it."

I snorted. "Evie practically tackled you in front of the whole town."

Jaxson lifted a brow.

"Tackled me? Yeah, right. More like she sprayed me with magical mace, gave me the silent treatment like I was some kind of awful ex, and then hexed my zipper shut when she turned me down the first few times. Hell, I earned my happily ever after."

"Sounds romantic," I muttered, rubbing my face.

"It was," he said smugly. "So what's your game plan with Donny? Or are you just planning on flexing your biceps near the bakery until she notices?"

I grunted.

"If that worked, she'd be mine already. I bake. I fight fires. I rescued her from literal divine lightning. And still? Nothing. Nada. Zip."

Jaxson grinned.

"So, you're saying she's immune to charm, heroics, and carbs? Damn, she really is powerful."

"I don't know what to do," I admitted, hating how

defeated I sounded. "I'm big, I'm awkward, I don't know anything about hair or fashion or whatever the heck she's into. And she's just so—"

"Deadly?" Jaxson offered.

"Sweet. Beautiful," I said.

"Scary," Jaxson said at the same time.

I gave him a look.

"Come on, man. You've met her, right? That Witch could melt titanium with her sass. She made a vending machine cry last week because it ate her dollar."

Before I could do more than snarl my response, *thump*—Conrad strolled in like he'd just slithered out of a sauna.

Shirtless. Again.

What was with Snake Shifters and their aversion to clothes?

"Don't kill the Wolf," the Python drawled lazily. "He's the Sheriff now, remember? We're supposed to be integrating."

"I wasn't gonna kill him," I grunted.

"Good. So. You want Donny's attention?" Conrad said, heading straight for the fridge.

"No, I'm just emotionally torturing myself for fun," I snapped.

Conrad pulled out a leftover meatball sub and waved it like a conductor's baton.

"Then stop being a dumbass. You want to get her attention? Get her alone."

"Sure. Great. I'll just accidentally trap her in an elevator next time we're both at Town Hall."

Jaxson snorted.

"Not the worst idea. Made me some fine memories in that elevator."

"Oh my fuck, shut up. I think I might hurl."

Lucky for me, Conrad ignored us both and continued.

"She's a stylist, dipshit. She owns a salon."

"And?" I raised a brow.

"And you look like a lumberjack who lost a bet. Go get a haircut. A shave too while you're at it."

"Huh?"

"Are all Bears slow? Book an appointment, son. Sit your ass in her chair and give her thirty uninterrupted minutes of Bear Shifter intensity. Hit her with all that growly goodness up close and personal."

Jaxson snapped his fingers.

"Conrad's got a point. You're a hot mess. Let Donny work her magic on you."

I blinked. "You think she'd go for that?"

"Think?" Conrad said. "I know. Women like

Donny want to feel useful. You show up looking like a sexy yeti and ask for help? That's bait, my man."

"And bonus," Jaxson added, "You'll finally stop looking like you escaped from a log cabin in the woods where you've been writing angry poetry and collecting beard oil."

I flipped them both off but couldn't stop the slow, creeping grin that took over my face.

"Fine. I'll make the damn appointment."

"Good," Conrad said. "Just don't let her shave off your eyebrows in revenge. You did hose her down with cold water in front of half the town."

I groaned.

"Fuck me."

Jaxson slapped my shoulder. "You're gonna be fine, Ry. Just try not to growl during the shampoo. That's how I got banned from two salons back in Colorado."

And that was how I found myself scheduling a haircut with the Witch of my dreams, praying I wouldn't accidentally shift when she touched my scalp.

Freaking hell.

What could possibly go wrong?

CHAPTER SIX-DONNY

THE NEXT DAY started out like any other—*which, in my world, meant a small domestic disaster was at least probable, but I was riding the high of optimism.*

First, coffee.

Always coffee.

I shuffled into the kitchen of my slightly haunted bungalow in my favorite silk pajamas and fuzzy bunny slippers (glam meets cozy), hair in a dark pineapple bun, and muttered my daily mantra.

"If the Goddess loves me, the coffee will be strong, and the Ghosts will keep quiet till noon."

The kettle went on.

I scooped a cup full of rich, dark Colombian beans—*roasted locally by a Fire Fae who may or may not be in a polycule (a romantic entanglement I don't think I could survive though I did ask about it once) with two Banshees and a disgraced Cupid*—and dumped them into my grinder.

The second I hit the button and that glorious *vrrrmmmmmm* filled the air, I moaned like the heroine in one of those spicy paperbacks Stanley, Bella and I passed around like contraband.

There is nothing—*nothing*—like that first hit of fresh coffee bean aroma.

Forget spellwork.

This was the *real magic.*

Now, don't get me wrong.

I know those little pod things are all the rage, but I refuse.

Sacrilege.

Coffee deserves foreplay.

It deserves effort.

So I grabbed my pour-over carafe and waited patiently for the water to boil like the classy, caffeinated Witch I was.

Exactly ten minutes later, I held the steaming chalice of my salvation.

I added two teaspoons of Italian sweet cream (non-negotiable), steered clear of the sugar, and last, added a delicate dash of cinnamon.

Perfect. Flawless. Sublime.

I took a sip and made a noise that probably summoned at least three lust Demons to my doorstep.

"Oh, baby," I whispered to the mug like it was my ex who'd just gotten hot and realized he was wrong.

Now, before you start asking, I didn't do sweeteners in my beverages—never had, never will.

I preferred my sugar to come in the form of something fried or baked and preferably filled with fruit or cream.

Like the decadent cherry turnover with triple berry icing I planned to inhale on the way to work.

It was already boxed and ready to go on the kitchen counter like a faithful feline friend—*the kind of familiar I should have been given instead of the furry little freak I'd been shackled to, but that was a complaint for another day.*

Right then, I had better things to think about than Gryn the Domodork.

Like coffee.

Rich, delicious, life-giving coffee.

Come to mama.

It was the start of a brand new work week, which meant the salon schedule was packed with my usuals.

Mrs. Yao wanted another perm (her third this

quarter), Ms. Furlong needed her root touchup (again).

The Chickee twins were due for synchronized haircuts.

And cranky old man Carol was coming in for a shave and a gossip sesh about the Werewolf HOA drama.

The man had opinions.

I sipped my coffee while scanning my phone.

Thank the Goddess for enchanted smartphones!

Mine had a specialty app that synced to my salon's bookings, weather ward alerts, lunar cycle forecasts, and local gossip threads.

WitchTok, who?

My assistant, Celeste (half Elf, half Gremlin, full chaotic magical energy), had access too, which meant changes happened in real time.

I trusted her. Well, mostly.

But then I saw the two last-minute appointments she'd added to my calendar this week, and I choked.

First up, Evie. Now, I loved the woman with all my heart, but the woman was simply boring when it came to her hair.

Only what was this?

She wanted highlights.

Highlights. Ooooh.

This was monumental.

I mean, here was a Witch who treated her hair like a national treasure and didn't even own a flat iron.

If she wanted to mess with the color, she must be deeply in love or completely unhinged.

Knowing how things were with her and Jaxson, I was guessing it was probably both.

Okay, so first new appointment, not so bad.

But the second one?

That's when the agita hit.

Yes. Agita.

If you're not Italian American, let me enlighten you.

Agita is that soul-deep, stomach-churning, throat-clenching, heart-fluttering mix of stress, indigestion, and irrational emotional distress that makes you want to scream, sob, and possibly fight someone. Or eat cake. Or both.

In layman's terms? Magical heartburn, baby.

And *yes*, I used it correctly. So, don't come at me.

And *no*, I didn't learn it from Drusilla's Witchy World Language Video Tutorials™, tagline: "You too can speak like an Orc and curse like a Warrior Princess!"—*although, let the record show, I am a loyal subscriber.*

Drusilla Bartholomew Frankenstein Yaganova is a national treasure. Period. Full stop.

Her tutorials are part educational, part spiritual awakening, and part chaotic disaster.

Think Martha Stewart meets Elvira in a haunted YouTube studio with low lighting and zero editing skills.

She's been referred to as "unfiltered brain soup for the up-and-coming magic user," which is honestly the best review I've ever read.

She also holds the supernatural world record for "most accidental familiars summoned on camera," and is besties with Magdelena—yes, the Magdelena, La Befana herself, and this year's likely Coven Award winner for Best Witch Who Does Not Accidentally Set Her Broom on Fire While Trying to Cleanse It.

Icons. Legends.

Both of them.

I follow their supernatural socials religiously—*like, actual candle-on-the-altar level devotion.*

Because those two? They've got more secrets than a Vampire's search history after a blood moon rave.

Anyway, back to the cause of my agita.

Ryan McLeod.

Firefighter. Baker. Behemoth. Bear.

A walking, talking carbohydrate with shoulders the size of a Buick and a voice so deep it could trigger an earthquake.

The kind of man who looks like he could throw you over his shoulder, carry you up a mountain, build you a cabin, and then make you cinnamon rolls from scratch while whispering sweet nothings into your very flushed ears.

So yeah. Agita. Lots of it. Right in the chest.

Fork my ever-loving life.

I nearly burned my tongue on my scalding hot coffee when I saw his name. And just like that, my perfectly calm morning turned into a full-blown emotional crisis.

Because after last night's firehose incident and the whole *smoking-hot-Shifter-douses-me-in-cold-water* humiliation, I was not ready for round two.

Unfortunately, the Universe didn't care.

Golden sparks zapped from my fingertips like I was some deranged magical Tinkerbell on a caffeine bender.

My beautiful coffee carafe tipped over, splashing its dark nectar of the gods everywhere.

"Goddess!" I groaned, slapping a dish towel over the mess like it was going to fix anything.

Then I paused.

I had just screamed the G-word with enough emotion to warrant *punishment*.

I looked up at the ceiling.

"Goddess, I did not mean that," I whispered. "I swear. Well. Not *swear* swear. I mean, I promise. That's better."

My neck craned as I peeked toward the rafters, fully expecting another pink lightning bolt of divine judgment to fry my butt like last time.

A snort brought my attention to the very short, very hairy nuisance I'd been stuck with for the past few weeks.

Gryn, *my freaky familiar*, actually hated me.

He shook his head at me, mumbling something in Polish, or Croatian, or maybe Russian—I had no idea.

And if I needed any actual physical confirmation that he disliked me intensely, well, he'd been leaving turds in my shoes, there's that.

Yep, actual turds. Glowing green, sometimes orange, and always horribly stinky turds.

It was all I could do not to try to blast him to pieces.

Truth was, the little fu—um *forker*, that's right—the little *forker* was powerful. Used to be worshiped as a minor household god or something like that.

Anyway, I just ignored his furry butt and continued with my conversation.

"Please believe me, Goddess, I am so very fuc—*forking* sorry. Forking. That's it! That's the word now!"

I pressed a hand to my chest and tried to breathe like Bella taught me in that one yoga class we did before we realized downward dog made our boobs try to suffocate us.

"Goddess on high, I promise to do my best to not swear and to be a true and courteous Witch. Please do not *fork* with my day any more than it is already *forked*."

Honestly, it was becoming a theme.

The Divine didn't care much for vulgarity, especially from magicals.

And apparently the Goddess was multilingual.

Evie heard it from La Befana herself.

The Goddess was also known as *She Who Must Not Be F-Bombed*.

According to Drusilla's vlog (which I watched like a religious soap opera), the Goddess was fluent in Italian, French, Latin, Greek, and Mandarin.

That eliminated 90% of my foul-mouthed arsenal. I was down to using kitchen utensils and onomatopoeia.

So here I was.

Caffeinated.

Flustered.

Slightly damp from the coffee incident.

And repeating the word "fork" like I was possessed by a Betty Crocker Demon.

Forkity fork fork fork.

I shook my head and placed my mug in the sink. As a result of my unfortunate coffee tragedy (RIP, magical brown elixir), I was now operating on approximately half my regular caffeine intake.

Which, for a normal human, might be fine.

But I was not normal.

I was a curvy, caffeinated chaos Witch running on glitter, sarcasm, and exactly 16 ounces of dark roast.

Luckily, salvation was just a short broom-ride—*er, walk*—away at Bella's bakery.

The Tasty Tart had everything a growing Witch needed.

Sugar, carbs, sass, and espresso shots strong enough to revive the dead.

Or at least reanimate my motivation.

My alarm buzzed from the living room, and I jumped like someone had set off a hex bomb.

"Fuh—" I started to yell before slapping a hand

over my mouth and glancing nervously toward the heavens.

I saw a pink crackle. Or two. And I cringed.

"I mean, forking hell!" I hissed. "I'm gonna be late!"

I scrambled to my bedroom like a poltergeist was chasing me.

I'd already wasted fifteen minutes mourning my coffee, and now I had approximately seven minutes to transform myself into a salon goddess before the doors of *Hair Now, Gone Tomorrow* opened for business.

Yes, that was the name of my shop.

Pun absolutely intended.

What can I say? I'm a sucker for wordplay and dramatic flair.

My regulars knew me as a top-tier stylist with a talent for layering both hair and trauma responses.

Sure, I had my share of male clients—*usually the laid-back type or the ones married to my friends*—but they were few and far between.

So what in the sparkly hell was he doing booking a last-minute trim?

Ryan McLeod was starting to be a real thorn in my side.

Seven feet of gruff, muscular, beard-sporting

Shifter with arms like tree trunks and a scowl like a Viking warlord who'd lost his ax.

The man had no business being that attractive. Or that big. Or that *growly*.

And now he was coming to me? For a haircut? Why?

Had Bella run out of Bear-sized croissant orders and forced him into a grooming intervention?

I pulled open my supply drawer and eyed my clippers.

Nope. Not good enough.

That beard of his looked like it had its own zip code.

If I was going to tackle that facial forest and the mop of shaggy curls on his head, I'd need divine intervention.

Or at least some high-power magical tools.

Raising one eyebrow, I considered summoning the Wahl Professional 5-Star Detailer—*a cordless legend in the hairstyling community, known to make even the surliest Shifters purr like pampered Pomeranians.*

But alas, enchanting professional-grade equipment without the proper permit was a punishable offense.

And the last thing I needed was a visit from the Magical Licensing Board.

Again.

I closed the drawer with a sigh.

Nope. No magical smuggling today.

I'm going in raw.

Oh my Goddess. I heard it as soon as I thought it.

My cheeks heated.

My girly bits perked up.

Even my nipples got hard.

"Nope. Nope. Absolutely not. That's a bad sentence," I muttered, smacking my forehead.

Because of course my brain went there.

Pull it together, Donny.

I could do this. I was a professional. I could give this giant walking temptation a haircut without flinging myself into his lap and begging him to braid my hair and tell me I'm pretty.

Probably.

And let's be honest—anything I did would be an improvement over what Doc from the old-timey barbershop down on Willow Street had to offer.

That man was still out here giving Elvis pompadours and calling it modern.

His musical taste was killer, though.

I'd never say no to a little Sinatra.

Today, however, I was feeling a bit more gangsta Witch.

I popped in my AirPods and let Tupac bless me with West Coast magic while I slipped on my most Witch-chic outfit.

Black skinny jeans, a deep purple tank top, and my favorite leather ankle boots.

Add in a smear of dark plum lipstick and a protective sigil drawn in eyeliner on my collarbone?

Bam. Ready for battle.

I took a deep breath, then another.

I had made a promise to keep my language clean and my hexes to a minimum.

I needed all the divine goodwill I could get if I was going to survive this week's surprise appointments.

Because Ryan McLeod?

He was not just a firehouse-flipping, croissant-baking, mountain-of-a-man problem.

He was *my* problem.

The man had only ever said, like, eight words to me since crashing into our town with his two equally uninvited friends.

And somehow in that time, he'd managed to do the improbable.

He'd seen me naked.

Given me a ride on his Bear—not a euphemism, although we could change that real quick.

And he'd hosed me down like an overexcited Dalmatian at the county fair.

Honestly, if he wasn't madly in love with me by now, I didn't know what else I could do.

Yeah. Right.

I rolled my eyes and grabbed my salon bag. This wasn't a romance novel.

The big, broody Bear wasn't going to fall on his knees and declare his undying love while running his fingers through my non-existent split ends.

Nope.

This was not a fairytale.

I was a Witch.

He was a Shifter.

And this was going to be the most awkward haircut of my entire forking life.

Let the chaos begin.

And that, dear diary, was how my morning started. Again.

CHAPTER SEVEN-DONNY

I WAS TRYING VERY HARD NOT to think about Ryan.

Like, Olympian-level mental gymnastics kind of trying. The kind of trying that required breathing exercises, scented candles, and the strongest anti-thirst spell I knew (which, for the record, didn't work—thanks a lot, Aunt Mimsy).

For the entire day, in fact, I'd been laser-focused on not thinking about Ryan McLeod, Bear Shifter and walking lumberjack fantasy.

But alas, my efforts were in vain.

Case in point, I accidentally added blue to Mrs. Niedermeyer's hair dye and turned her platinum locks into a not-so-subtle shade of grape popsicle. Violet freaking reign.

Thankfully, Mrs. Niedermeyer was enchanted with her new look. Said it brought out her *inner seductress* and asked if I could make her eyebrows match next week.

Then she called me a genius and tottered off in her orthopedic pumps like she was headed to a red carpet event.

I, on the other hand, was barely holding on.

The Bear was in my head. Again. Him and his thick, overgrown mane of hair.

No matter what I did—*spritzed detangler, burned sage, or dunked my face in a tub of glitter slime*—there he was.

Creeping up in my thoughts like a bad cowlick that refused to stay down.

Ugh, but what could I do?

Ever since the garden hose incident, I simply couldn't stop.

Not after he'd caught me mid-swear, mid-fireball, and mid-freakout in front of half the town. I still had nightmares about that moment.

He'd just stood there, calm as a boulder in a stream, while I melted down like a toddler who missed nap time.

I needed control.

Composure.

A shot of espresso.

And some age-defying moisturizer, stat.

Not feelings.

And definitely not a Bear Shifter who looked like Paul Bunyan's hotter, moodier cousin with a six-pack and bedroom eyes that made my knees wobble like undercooked spaghetti.

"Celeste!" I barked, storming out of the back room.

She looked up from her phone, where she was watching what I can only assume was a tutorial on how to summon a glamour spell using only eyelash glue and a dream.

"Yes, boss lady?"

"I need to go next door for snacks. Emergency."

She blinked. "Oh no. Is it blood sugar? Magic deficiency? Existential crisis?"

"Yes," I snapped. "All of the above. And also, I'm spiraling, and if I don't shove a maple-glazed donut in my face in the next five minutes, I might accidentally turn you into a turnip."

Celeste gasped. "Again?!"

"Just watch the register," I said, snatching my purse. "And if anyone comes in asking for a same-day balayage, tell them to walk directly into the sea."

"But the sea is at least twenty-two blocks away!"

"Then they'll have time to reflect on their bad decisions," I called, already halfway out the door.

I needed sugar, caffeine, and a break from the very large, very hairy man who had somehow become the main character in every single one of my waking fantasies.

Also, maybe a cinnamon twist.

Gold sparkles danced along my fingertips, and I closed my eyes and counted to five before walking out the door.

Keeping my powers in check was part of the job. As one-third of the magical Witch Trifecta that guarded Castor's Corner, I had responsibilities.

Big ones.

It was my job to keep our cozy, Witchy little town from turning into a supernatural theme park for tourists.

This was a haven. A sanctuary. A glittering Jersey gem for Witches, Shifters, Fae, and even the occasional grumpy Troll.

Everything was fine until recently. When we went and forked it all up.

I am talking big time forked up.

Our magical protections had failed, our rituals had been interrupted, and worst of all, some kids had gotten stolen. Oh, and our graveyard had been actually haunted.

Although the latter turned out to be *Evie's dead grandpa,* who, plot twist, also turned out to be *my* grandpa. And Bella's.

Yep. That old warlock had gotten around more than a Black Friday sales flyer.

Which meant Evie, Bella, and I weren't just best friends—we were *family.*

Blood sisters.

Literally.

Turns out, Grandpa Al was like the Casanova of the Witch world, leaving behind a trail of magical DNA.

I could sense some seriously awkward family reunions in my near future—*and didn't that suck?*

I mean, the old man had been busier than a broom on Halloween.

So yeah, the last few weeks have been busy as fork.

I had a lot of information to process.

Family secrets.

Sexy Shifters.

Work—there was always work drama.

And don't even get me started on my grandmother.

That sanctimonious old Witch used to lecture me about my miniskirts and my *fast behavior*, all while she was out there playing magical hide the wand with someone else's man.

Talk about the cauldron calling the kettle scandalous.

But where did all this leave me?

I'll tell you where. On line at The Tasty Tart, adding another inch to my already rotund ass—thanks to Aunt Edna who was apparently my relative now, too.

And was it worth it?

I sighed as I grabbed my order, shoved a bite of baked goodness into my mouth, and stomped back to my salon.

Geezus, that was good.

What the heck was Bella putting in this stuff—chocolate crack?

Anyway, the answer was yes.

Yes, it was worth it.

CHAPTER EIGHT-DONNY

MY THOUGHTS CONTINUED to swirl around my head as I walked and chewed.

The past was done, right? I should let it go.

I mean, Grandpa Al was gone, onto the *Next Amazing Journey*—just one of several *Witchy euphemisms for the great beyond.*

Grandma was probably judging angels now.

And I had more important things to worry about —like how the hell we were going to fix the real problem, i.e. whatever was draining our wards so quickly, so that we could protect our town before something *really* nasty snuck in.

So yes, we'd messed up a bonfire.

It was supposed to be a full moon strip-and-cast

ceremony—*your standard naked dance around a fire under the stars kind of thing.*

You know, just another weekday for a Jersey Witch.

But Evie had been late, Bella forgot the rosemary (again), and I had been mid-curse when the Goddess herself decided to zap my ass with a lightning bolt of divine disapproval. Which, *ow.*

Okay, so Evie did solve some of the crap that cropped up—like outing her ex-boyfriend Dickless Dick as the idiot not-so-mastermind behind a weak plot to seize mayorship from her.

Also, we saved some kids, which was all like *yay.*

But for the last few weeks we've been stumped. No progress had been made at all.

And this morning?

Well, let's just say the streak was continuing.

My magic was twitchy, my familiar was a no-show (except when he needed to defecate, which apparently, he only did in my shoes, the little cretin), caffeine was underwhelming, and I had a whole list of appointments and things to see to at the salon that included—*gulp*—*Ryan McLeod himself.*

I still couldn't wrap my head around the fact that the Bear Shifter wanted an appointment with me.

By personal request, if the note Celeste jotted down was true.

Hint: It was.

Ryan wants to see me.

Oh. My. Gaia.

Butterflies? Please. I had a whole fleet of combat drones doing aerial maneuvers in my stomach. They were dropping magical anxiety bombs and glittery confetti like they were on parade duty.

This was getting out of hand.

Ridiculous, even.

I couldn't believe one oversized bearded Bear Shifter had me more wound up than a teenager waiting to be asked to prom—which, by the way, totally sucked.

I mean, if we're being honest here—*and when am I not*—I asked out the foreign exchange student because he was cute, mysterious, and had a magical accent.

Also, the local options were meh.

What I didn't realize? He was a Wombat Shifter going through his first heat cycle.

Yep. Heat. Cycle.

The boy spent the entire night attempting to twerk me into submission on the dance floor.

And I don't mean cute, club-style twerking. I

mean violent, territorial, possibly ancestral Wombat-wooing gyrations that nearly threw out my lower back and summoned a Lust Demon from the astral plane.

It was like Dirty Dancing if Patrick Swayze had been replaced by an over-caffeinated marsupial.

But hey, how was I supposed to know it was some sort of mating ritual?

I just wanted to dance and eat my weight in finger sandwiches.

Not end up betrothed to a sweaty exchange student with a pouch.

Never again.

Anyway, back to the present and my current existential crisis.

Ryan McHotStuff McLeod wanted me to cut his hair.

Just a haircut. Totally normal. Professional. Harmless.

Lies. All lies.

Because I knew when that man sat in my chair, all broad shoulders and smoldering bear eyes and massive thighs that made my salon smock feel like lingerie?

My brain was going to short-circuit faster than my curling iron during a thunderstorm.

Calm the fork down, Donny. It's just a haircut. Not other things.

Not that I'd mind the other things. If he offered them.

Casually.

Respectfully.

Shirtlessly.

FOCUS.

I clapped my hands together like I was breaking a spell. Because I probably was.

Haircut. That's all.

Snip snip, Bear boy. Snip snip.

I took a deep breath, fluffed my locks, and told myself for the hundredth time that I could handle this.

I was a Witch, damn it. A powerful one. A *professional.*

I just hoped the Goddess didn't decide to zap me again if Ryan said something grumbly and sexy and I accidentally let an f-bomb fly.

Because let's be real—*I was definitely gonna fork that up.*

Anyway, where was I?

Oh yeah. Munching and walking at the same time. Kudos to me.

So, it's Fall. Autumn.

Weeks after what the town lovingly referred to as the Witch Trifecta's latest little mishap. And you know, the usual was happening.

Cinnamon scented chaos to take in.

Updates on our pecker-happy Grandpa Al to be found.

Magical misfires to correct.

And Zap-happy Goddesses to avoid.

I should have been happy that I managed to miss a certain smexy Grizzly at The Tasty Tart.

Lucky me, right?

Only I felt disappointment rather than relief.

What was wrong with me?

I was already headed back to the salon, looking forward to imbibing some of the hot coffee and crumbly deliciousness I'd acquired, but of course the universe had other designs.

I readjusted my oversized sunglasses as I strolled down Main Street, purse in one hand and my newly filled travel mug in the other.

The crisp air smelled like cinnamon brooms and crunchy leaves, and despite my general aversion to sunshine and happiness—*and, let's be honest and add responsibility to my list of aversions*—I had to admit it was pretty forking glorious outside.

The shops along the street had begun to decorate

for the Fall Harvest Bash, which, in Castor's Corner, meant the following.

Pumpkins.

Pumpkins everywhere.

Some with smiles, some with fangs, one that winked at me every time I passed, and I swear I'm not imagining it.

Apple cider stands popping up like magical zits.

Cobwebs—*real and fake*—decorating every corner.

The real ones courtesy of the local Spider Shifters, who saw the season as their time to shine.

And of course, an alarming uptick in basic Witches trying to sneak pumpkin spice spells into every baked good within reach.

Note to self: Talk to Bella about the incident from last year.

She'd sold *bake-at-home* muffin kits, which—*when in the hands of some of these supes who insisted on adding too much pumpkin spice to the already perfect recipe*—accidentally got a little out of control.

See, the muffins were magicked with just the right amounts of every ingredient, and when more got added to the mix, well, they did everything from levitating to moaning for hours.

Some actually exploded, destroying an entire *cul de sac* in one instance.

I took a bite of a chocolate croissant with mocha icing—*no, it didn't last very long*—and moaned as sugary goodness trailed down my fingers like glitter from the heavens.

While I chewed, I tried to ignore the prickle of awareness crawling down my spine.

There it was again.

That sensation.

Like someone was watching me.

Thinking about me.

Obsessing over me, maybe.

My nipples did not need this level of alertness on an average afternoon, *thank you very much.*

It wasn't a bad feeling, exactly.

Not like the one I got when our wards hiccupped, or when a Demon accidentally slipped into the dry cleaners and turned all the dress shirts into crop tops.

No, this felt *warm*. Tingly. Like someone had dipped my aura in chocolate fondue and whispered, "Dessert's served."

No prizes for guessing who it was.

Ryan. Forking. McLeod.

The brooding Bear firefighter-baker who

haunted my dreams like a sexy carbs-and-lumber-jack-themed Ghost.

Ever since he and his shifty Shifter bros crash-landed in our town like a supernatural boy band on a bender, things had been complicated.

Sure, Evie was all paired up, and even Bella was starry-eyed now.

And sure, the wards had started purring again like a well-fed kitten.

But me? I was still single. Still frazzled. Still trying not to set my eyebrows on fire every time Ryan looked at me like he wanted to lick icing off my soul.

And speaking of licking.

No. Nope. Fork no.

Not going there. My hormones had enough fuel without adding Bear Boy's buns to the mix.

Still, it was a truth universally acknowledged that I was deeply, undeniably, frustratingly attracted to the man.

And did he notice? *Probably.*

Did he care? *Unclear.*

The guy made sourdough look like a less compli-cated rise-and-fall situation than the tension between us.

Which brought me back to the whole Fated Mates theory.

Ugh.

There was something about the way Ryan looked at me.

Not with lust (although that definitely factored in), but with this quiet, unwavering certainty that unnerved me more than a pixie on espresso.

Like he knew something I didn't.

Like maybe he'd already made up his mind.

Like he was just waiting for me to catch up.

Honestly? Rude.

I mean, come on.

How was I supposed to function when I had none of the info?

How was I supposed to get my concentration back when the man baked pastries like they were love letters and smelled like bourbon, vanilla, and campfire?

With great difficulty, that's how.

My phone pinged, and I looked down at an incoming text message from Evie.

Uh oh.

It was marked urgent, and I knew what that meant.

Disaster was likely about to strike, but that was nothing new.

I kept on walking, determined to keep my cool.

After all, I was Donatella Andrews, thank you very much.

Local legendary stylist. Co-leader of the town's magical defense squad. Hair goddess. And proud owner of a drawer full of high-end vibrators and zero regrets.

Okay.

Maybe one regret.

That I hadn't kissed him when I'd had the chance. That time he'd accidentally-on-purpose flour-dusted me at the bakery and offered to lick it off my fingers. I'd nearly combusted on the spot.

But I didn't kiss him.

Instead, I ran.

Like a chicken.

A magical chicken in cute boots.

Why? Because if I let myself fall, *really fall*, I wasn't sure I'd ever get back up.

Ryan wasn't just some hot hookup or crush.

My magic knew it.

My gut knew it.

My freaking ovaries were sending engraved invitations.

But my heart? She'd been through some shiz, okay?

She was cautious. She was a little bruised. And she wasn't looking to get dragged through the romantic wringer without backup.

Besides, if this whole Fated Mate situation turned out to be one big cosmic prank, I'd have to get Evie to hold my earrings while I cursed the Goddess herself.

Speaking of Evie, I spotted her outside the flower shop, waving me down like a lunatic.

"I brought snacks!" I yelled, lifting my turnover like it was a peace offering.

She grinned and held up her coffee.

"I brought caffeine. Bella's bringing scarves—she's knitting again."

"Oh no," I said, slapping a hand over my mouth.

"Come on. Let's go save the town."

"Again?"

She shrugged. "You know the drill."

And I did.

Because no matter how messy, dramatic, or downright weird life in Castor's Corner got, I had my girls.

I had my town. And they had me.

And honestly?

That was enough—*for now.*

CHAPTER NINE-RYAN

OKAY, so hear me out.

I wasn't stalking Donny.

I was simply *observing* her general vicinity in a highly protective and mildly obsessive fashion from a totally safe, respectful distance.

You know. *Like a gentleman.*

Listen, I'm a Shifter, not a Warlock—*or Wizard or Sorcerdude or whatever the heck the male version of a Witch is these days*—but I knew when something was off. And something was definitely wrong in Castor's Corner.

The town was humming with weird energy. Like, more than usual.

Jaxson, who was now our official Sheriff and

unofficial King of Smug Mated Wolves, had been muttering about activity at the cemetery again.

Ghosts stirring.

Shadows moving.

Creepy cold spots popping up where cold spots should not be.

And as the closest thing this town had to a functioning Fire Chief—*okay, technically it's Acting Fire Captain, but who's checking titles*—I'd been looped in on more of the local weirdness than I ever thought possible when I applied for a simple job helping people not spontaneously combust.

Now I was dealing with haunted grocery stores, exploding glam spells, and Wererats forming a drum circle behind the laundromat. It was a lot.

But the real reason my Bear was pacing like a caffeinated linebacker inside my chest?

Donny.

Donny freaking Andrews.

Witch. Goddess. Chaos tornado wrapped in curves and snark and fireball energy.

She was part of the town's magical Trifecta— *along with Evie and Bella*—three badass Witches tasked with keeping our supernatural haven safe.

And every time I looked at her, I felt something

ancient rumble in my soul like an avalanche of fate and pheromones.

Yeah. My Bear was convinced she was mine.

Not in a creepy, possessive *you belong to me now* way—though let's be honest, I wouldn't say no if she decided she belonged to me voluntarily—but in the *I will throw hands with the entire underworld if she so much as stubs her toe* kind of way.

So when Jaxson casually mentioned something *unusual* stirring in the cemetery—*new Ghost, maybe the old one doing interpretive dance again*—I knew Donny would be the first to march in, spellbook in one hand and iced coffee in the other.

I also knew she'd downplay it.

Act like she had it handled.

Because she always did.

But even the strongest Witch deserved backup.

So yeah, when I saw her walk into The Tasty Tart during my shift, all hips and sass and hair that made me want to bury my face in it for the rest of my life, I may have slipped out the back.

Casually. Quietly.

Then shifted into my fur.

And padded through the trees lining Main Street, keeping a respectful distance while she walked back toward her salon.

Call me crazy.

I call it caring enthusiastically.

I didn't growl.

I didn't drool.

I didn't even sniff the air like some hormonal teenager on his first heat.

Okay, maybe I did sniff the air a little.

She smells like wildflower honey, and Witchy temptation. You try resisting that.

But here's the truth. I'm crazy about her.

Like, absolutely unhinged for this woman who doesn't even know how hard she's hit me.

My Bear is ready to mate for life.

Me? I'm just hoping she'll let me buy her a coffee and maybe brush her hair someday.

Fuck you. It's not creepy.

In the meantime, I'll be here.

Waiting. Watching.

Not stalking—*strategically protecting.*

Just in case some new Ghost or Ghoul decides to get froggy.

Because no one messes with my Witch.

Not on my watch.

CHAPTER TEN-DONNY

OKAY, so I managed to avoid the furry giant for the last few days, which honestly should've qualified me for some kind of magical endurance medal.

But it looked like my luck—*and my caffeine reserves*—had officially run out.

Celeste, bless her color-clashing little heart, is to blame for all of this.

For my last few sleepless nights. And my agita.

This mother-humping agita that's making me regret eating the raspberry preserve-slathered rye toast I had this morning.

Him.

Ryan McLeod.

The Grizzly Godzilla who haunted my dreams, my fantasies, and the one time I got caught sniffing a cinnamon roll that suspiciously smelled like his beard.

He was booked for a haircut. With me.

And it was for tonight.

The last slot of the day, which was usually reserved for my favorite clients—*aka the ones who tipped well, didn't try to flirt, and didn't stare at my boobs like they were enchanted talismans.*

So, yeah. This was my life now.

Thanks a fork-ton, Celeste.

I contemplated letting out a primal scream or possibly whacking her upside the head with a rolled-up copy of Witch *Weekly*, but I controlled myself.

Barely. *Or was it bearly?*

Ugh, I was already punning, and he wasn't even in the chair yet.

I needed more caffeine. Stat.

Celeste, for all her magical potential, had the attention span of a fruit bat on espresso.

The young, glitter-obsessed Witch had just hit her second decade of life and believed crop tops were a personality trait.

Her hair was currently the color of a Montana sky at high noon, and her eyebrows? Hot pink lightning bolts.

Because of course they were.

She dreamed of being a famous influencer—posting spells on WitchTok and trying to get sponsored by cauldron brands that hadn't been relevant since the fifties. I didn't mind her hanging around.

She was a decent shampoo tech, a disaster with the appointment book, and apparently allergic to sweeping.

Still. She meant well. I guessed.

No, the real menace to my peace, my sanity, and my favorite sweater was currently in the living room, unraveling said sweater like it was yarn spun from the hair of a blessed unicorn.

Gryn.

My so-called familiar.

Some joke that was. A familiar was supposed to make a Witch's life easier.

They were supposed to focus their Witch's magic.

To aid and temper.

Not annoy and destroy, for fork's sake.

But Gryn was simply a mangy, attitude-ridden ball of magical fur and judgment.

And because my life was a circus without a tent, he'd decided today was the perfect time to rediscover his love for obscure Eastern European punk rock.

From the eighties. Played at ear-bleeding decibels. On vinyl.

I swear on my stash of high-quality clippers, if he scratched another one of my records, I was going to toss him into the backyard and let the Garden Gnomes decide his fate.

My nerves were frazzled, and my hair was only seven out of ten today—*I know, right?*

What was the world coming to?

But I was in no shape to answer that question. No, I knew what I needed.

Coffee and chocolate.

Right forking now.

The line leading into The Tasty Tart, Bella's amazeballs bakery, was already wrapped around the corner like a glittering, colorful boa of townsfolk.

I huffed out a breath but refused to use my bestie privileges to cut.

That kind of chaos wasn't worth the calories, and besides, skipping the line at Bella's was basically asking to be hexed by a caffeine-deprived Dragon Shifter with control issues.

And I liked my skin un-molted, thank you very much.

I scanned the queue and counted. Three Coyotes in athleisure, two bickering Warlocks (probably still fighting over that shared familiar from last month), six Witches (three of whom were trying to pretend they hadn't just magically plucked their under-eye bags away), one twitchy Gopher Shifter in a trench coat, a Troll with rhinestone glasses, and two Fae arguing about gluten.

A colorful cast of characters, but this was Castor's Corner.

We were nothing if not festive in our dysfunction.

No way I was stepping in front of that group.

Bella would have the line moving faster than a Gnome on espresso.

According to the chalkboard sign in the window, the *chocolatey chippers* were the cookie of the week, and those babies were the stuff of legend.

Warm, gooey, sprinkled with fairy sugar and just enough attitude to bite back.

I'd wait. I could be patient. Mostly.

Besides, it gave me time to mentally prepare for the circus that was my Wednesday salon schedule.

Most people treated Thursdays like a happy Friday Eve. A precursor to a fun weekend.

But for me, it was the equivalent of magical DEFCON 1.

Thursdays signaled my busiest workdays were just beginning.

They were the prelude to prom updos, bachelorette hair emergencies, and last-minute shapeshifter grooming appointments from beings who forgot their high school reunion was tonight.

The wind whipped around the corner, sending goosebumps skittering up my arms. I shivered.

Of course, my mind went right to the fuzzy thief currently nesting in my favorite fall sweater.

That little fork-weasel.

Gryn, was technically a Domovyk. Ancient, mysterious, powerful.

In my case? Disrespectful, rude, and aggressively territorial over my wardrobe.

That rat-tailed, horn-headed menace had shredded the sleeves of my pumpkin spice cashmere and turned it into a makeshift nest in the middle of my living room wall.

Not near the wall.

Not against the wall.

In. The. Wall.

I'd woken up this morning to the sound of screeching punk rock blaring from what I could only guess was his ancient demonic Walkman, followed by the delicate sound of yarn unraveling in real time.

If I hadn't already downed half a cup of coffee, I might've committed a capital magical crime.

And Gryn? He'd just cackled like a Gremlin, spat some profanity in Domojerk, and bolted through the hallway dragging what used to be my sleeve behind him like a trophy.

"Damn Domovyks," I muttered, rubbing my temple and resisting the urge to call a spiritual exterminator.

Evie and Bella had lucked out.

Their familiars were perfect.

Evie got Ivan, who seemed to purr spells in his sleep and was always there for her. Seriously, those two were a force when they worked together.

And Bella? She had the sweetest little familiar in Petyr, who made perfect cupcakes with the best marshmallow frosting I ever had.

Me? I got a tiny Slavic trash goblin who threatened to shave my eyebrows in the middle of the night.

"Maybe I can trade him on eBay," I whispered, mostly to myself.

Magic flared in my fingertips at the thought, my anger pushing forward like a sneeze.

My hair, which I'd spent forty-five minutes

styling that morning, frizzed out around my head like an electrocuted lioness.

I patted it down and took a deep breath.

He wasn't worth getting zapped over. Again.

I had scars on my butt from the last magical rebound incident.

One little zap, one mispronounced banishment spell, and boom—week-long reminder that the Goddess has a wicked sense of humor and a zero-tolerance policy for accidental curses.

I groaned as I reached the front of the line and stepped inside, instantly wrapped in the scent of warm sugar, vanilla bean, and pure serotonin.

Heaven. Pure, delicious, belly-rumbling heaven.

I was so focused on the baked goods display case *—eyeballing a turnover that was definitely giving me the eye—*I didn't notice the figure behind the counter until he spoke.

"Can I help you?" a deep, rumbly voice asked, smoother than melted chocolate and just as dangerous.

I looked up and immediately regretted it.

Oh no.

There he was.

Ryan.

The. Bear. Shifter.

He had a jawline that could cut glass, arms like tree trunks, and the soulful brown eyes of a man who'd write poetry about your thighs. And he was wearing an apron that said "Bake It Til You Make It."

"Fork me," I muttered, eyes closing in embarrassment as my body flushed with a mix of heat, horror, and oh-for-the-love-of-all-things-magical why now?

When I opened them again, he was still there.

Still gorgeous.

Still not noticing that my brain had short-circuited from sheer proximity.

I cleared my throat and tried to act like a functional human Witch.

"One cherry turnover," I croaked. "Please."

"Just one?" he asked, lips twitching like he knew exactly the effect he had on me.

I raised an eyebrow and gave him my best don't-mess-with-me stare. "Unless one comes with a side of sanity and a new sweater, yes. Just one."

Ryan chuckled.

It was deep. Warm. And dangerously close to sounding like it belonged in my fantasies.

He handed me a wax paper bag and our fingers brushed.

Cue the fireworks.

Literally.

My fingertips sparked with a soft glow of magic, and a tiny static crackle popped in the air between us.

"Oh no," I whispered.

"Was that—?" he started.

"Nope!" I blurted. "Nothing. Static. It's dry out. Gotta go!"

And just like that, I turned and marched out of the bakery like it hadn't just turned into my personal shame spiral.

Fork. My. Life.

CHAPTER ELEVEN—RYAN

SHE WAS GONE in a flurry of hips, perfume, and sass.

Donny practically sprinted out of The Tasty Tart, clutching her turnover like it was a weapon and leaving me standing there with a smile I couldn't shake off my face.

Damn.

She was everything.

Curvy. Commanding. Chaotic in the most delicious way.

And totally, completely mine—if I believed for even one second, she'd ever give me a real chance.

My Bear? Oh, he believed.

He was pacing inside me like a damn caged

animal, grumbling at me for letting our mate escape. Again.

You let her leave, idiot. She sparked. We sparked. Claim her.

Yeah. Great plan, buddy.

Right after I win a Nobel Peace Prize for Shifters, and get the mop out for the magical explosion that would definitely follow.

I blew out a breath and rubbed the back of my neck, feeling that familiar ache settle in my chest.

The ache of *wanting.*

Of knowing who she was—*what she was*—to me, and not being able to do a damn thing about it.

"She zapped you again, didn't she?" Jaxson asked, strolling in through the back door, smug as ever.

"She did not," I grunted, but the static still dancing over my fingers gave me away.

Conrad was right behind him, arms crossed and smirking like he'd just seen a particularly juicy soap opera scene play out.

"Was it a little zap or one of those *kiss-me-or-die* level jolts?" Conrad asked, tilting his head. "Because if she fried your frontal lobe again, I call dibs on your croissant recipe."

"You two are the worst," I muttered, turning away

before either of them saw the dumb grin creeping back onto my face.

"She wants you, bro," Jaxson said, dragging a stool over and dropping onto it like he owned the place. "No sparks without a charge. It's basic supernatural physics."

"Is that a thing?" Conrad asked.

"It is now."

I shook my head and grabbed the towel off my shoulder, using it to wipe down the already spotless counter.

Anything to keep my hands busy.

Anything to keep from thinking about her scent lingering in the air—something warm and floral with a hint of honey and defiance.

"She doesn't want me," I muttered. "She avoids me like I'm a walking tax audit."

"She's scared," Conrad offered, surprisingly thoughtful. "You're a lot of Bear. And let's be honest, Donny's used to being the strongest person in the room."

That shut me up.

Because he wasn't wrong.

Donatella Andrews was the kind of woman who could shatter a man with her stare, then fix his whole damn life with a flick of her wrist and a perfectly timed hair appointment.

She ran a salon, wielded scissors like a sword, and kept this whole magical town safe with her two best friends.

She didn't need a mate.

She *chose* people.

And clearly, she hadn't chosen me yet.

But my Bear?

He was done waiting.

"You think when I show up for my haircut, she'll finally talk to me?" I asked, rubbing my jaw.

"Depends," Jaxson said. "Are you gonna tell her you're her fated mate while she's holding sharp objects?"

"No. I just thought maybe I'd ask her out."

"Okay, then. I say go for it," Conrad shrugged. "Worst case, you end up with a man bun and a wounded ego."

"Or no ears," Jaxson added.

I stared at my reflection in the bakery's glass case.

Beard like a forest fire.

Hair like a Bear who'd just rolled out of hibernation and lost a fight with a wind tunnel.

Yeah. It was time.

"I'm confirming my appointment," I said.

Conrad clapped me on the shoulder. "That's the spirit, you big lovesick biscuit."

Jaxson grinned. "Just don't growl when she touches your neck. That's how restraining orders happen."

I flipped them both off and grabbed the bakery phone.

Time to face the Witch.

And maybe—*just maybe*—win her over.

One trim at a time.

CHAPTER TWELVE-DONNY

AS SOON AS I ran out of the bakery guilt hit me like a hurricane wind.

I didn't even speak to Bella. Shit.

I grabbed my Witch approved smart phone and dialed the bakery line—which I had on speed dial.

"The Tasty Tart, this is Ryan," a deep voice said.

"HOLY FORK!"

"What was that?" Ryan asked, tone sounding bemused.

Of course, he didn't know it was me or that he just lit me up like a forking Yule log.

"Um, nothing. Can I speak to Bella?" I croaked, pretending I hadn't just semi-orgasmed from the sound of his rumbling, like a thirsty Succubus on day six of a juice cleanse.

"Sure. One second, she's in the back," he said, and I swear I could hear the hint of a smile just as easily as I could picture it beneath the beard and mustache that looked like they'd been kissed by the gods of rugged masculinity and sinful bedtime dreams.

Ugh. There I went again.

I squeezed my thighs together tighter than the last pair of skinny jeans I'd ever bought and immediately regretted.

Ryan McLeod was hotter than Luigi's Fra Diavolo special—*with double the heat and none of the regret*—unless you counted the ache between my legs every time he so much as breathed in my direction.

I gulped.

He growled into the receiver, and I swear the world tilted.

"Here she comes, but I'll see you later? For my appointment."

Oh, fork me sideways. He did know it was me.

His voice was low, grumbly, and just a little too intimate.

I nodded, which was dumb. Ryan couldn't see me over the phone, for fork's sake.

But I couldn't find my tongue.

Could not. Find. My. Tongue.

So naturally, I just kept on nodding like an unhinged bobblehead.

Smooth, Donny. Real smooth.

"I'll take your silence as a yes, Honey."

Then, he chuckled—*a low, masculine rumble that made my nipples harden beneath my bra.*

I listened as he called out for Bella like he hadn't just completely wrecked my day with a few measly words.

I mean, The Tasty tart was a daily stop for me.

But how the forking hell was I supposed to waltz past this bakery every morning now, knowing full well this man—*my possible, probable actual mate*—was inside slinging croissants and sex appeal like it was his job?

Inhale. Exhale.

No lightning.

That was good.

I was managing my profanity enough to avoid celestial punishment.

Small wins, girl. Small wins.

"Morning, Donny," Bella said.

She always sounded so happy and bright.

Like a damn Botticelli angel who'd traded in her harp for a mixing spoon.

The beyotch.

"For fork's sake, Bella, stop being so cheerful!" I snapped, more bark than bite.

She didn't even flinch. Just giggled with the patience of a thousand blessed bakers and cooed to me like I was a small child having a temper tantrum.

"Oh, so you are trying to stop cursing, *och*?" she said, and I could almost see her blue eyes twinkling.

I narrowed mine.

"Uh, yeah. And what's with the Orc? Are you listening to *Drusilla Bartholomew Frankenstein Yaganova's Language Vlog*, too?"

Bella paused.

"What?"

"You know, the one with the cursed name and the weekly affirmations in fourteen dialects? She has a whole episode about swearing substitutions. She calls it *sanitizing the soul.*"

"Donny, you need coffee. And something deep-fried. And covered in sugar," she said as if she were addressing an invisible council of Wise Pastry Elders.

Which was entirely possible.

It *was* Castor's Corner.

Something covered the receiver, and I heard

Bella speaking fondly to someone else. She mentioned Petyr, and I tried in vain to listen to their exchange.

Her tiny Domovyk familiar was the epitome of manners and helpfulness, while mine was pure evil incarnate.

He was always trotting about the bakery cleaning or cooking or with six trays of perfectly balanced baked goods in one freakishly strong hand.

He even waved politely to me whenever I saw him.

"Bella? Bella! Is that Petyr?" I shouted into the phone.

"Good morning, Lady Donatella," he said in his deep, old-timey accent, like we were at a royal court instead of a bakery.

"Yeah, Donny. Sorry, Petyr was just telling me about the funniest thing that happened when he went and delivered cookies to the elementary school this morning," Bella explained.

I took in her mirth and merriment with some-thing akin to shock.

"Okay, what the actual fork? He works for you? Voluntarily or you have to pay him in like your unborn children or something?" I asked.

"What? Oh my goodness, Donny, no! Petyr is amazing!"

She went on to explain his duties. Told me how he loved stocking shelves, wiping counters, and taking expert care of the stainless steel trays used to hold the baked goods she was famous for. He even spent his nights cleaning the kitchen.

From what she said and what I'd seen of Petyr, I knew he did all these things with so much grace he made *me* feel like an awkward rhinoceros in a thong.

"I just adore him," Bella said, and I could almost picture the little weirdo puffing out his chest like she'd handed him a damn Oscar.

I was also willing to bet he had all the shelves filled, the kitchen restocked, and not a single sprinkle out of place in the whole damn bakery.

"I don't understand. How do you do that?"

"Do what?"

"Your *Domofreak* isn't trying to destroy your bakery or pull your hair out? How?"

Bella gasped and probably clutched her pearls— or rather, her flour-dusted apron strap.

"First off, Donny, I don't call him demeaning names!"

"Oh, please. Gryn is a freaking monster with a Napoleon complex and a hair fetish. He yanked my ponytail this morning and called me a *cow* in Slovakian."

"You don't speak Slovakian," she said mildly.

"No, but I *felt* the insult in my soul," I snapped.

Bella giggled, and I could only imagine what Petyr was doing now. Probably serenading a tray of muffins.

"I don't know what to tell you. Petyr's a doll. Maybe if you were a little more—"

"Don't finish that sentence unless you want a hexed scone shoved up your—"

"Ladies, sorry to intrude, but the customers can hear you both through the phone," came Ryan's voice again through the receiver, deep and low, interrupting the world's most awkward familiar intervention.

I froze like a deer caught mid-lip gloss application.

Bella, of course, just spoke normally. "Thank you for the reminder, Ryan. Donny is a delight in the mornings, isn't she?"

"Totally," Ryan replied, and his voice went even deeper.

Oh, Goddess, help me.

I was going to die of spontaneous combustion

right there between the shampoo station and my shelf of conditioning masks.

All because of a Bear with bedroom eyes and a voice that melted my insides like hot sugar on a funnel cake.

Fork me sideways.

Yes, please!

CHAPTER THIRTEEN—DONNY

CELESTE WAS WAITING behind the front desk of *Hair Now, Gone Tomorrow* with a hopeful expression and a plate of oddly lumpy cookies.

"Want to try some peanut butter biscuits?" she asked, practically bouncing with excitement, which —*considering how tight her rhinestone-studded jeans were*—was a public safety hazard.

I gave the cookies a side-eye so judgmental it could've peeled wallpaper.

"Thanks, but better not. I've got the Chicky twins first thing."

"Ah," she nodded wisely. "Nut allergies. Good thinking. I can check the break room and see if there's something fruity and nut-free for you."

"It's fine," I lied smoothly. "I'm not hungry."

Lies.

Lies and slander.

I was always hungry.

But now was not the time to indulge.

Not with Denice and Candice Chickazola on the schedule.

Those two octogenarian hellcats were legendary in Castor's Corner—and not in a good way.

They were like the Sour Patch Kids of the supernatural community. Chaotic, terrifying, deceptively sweet-looking, and a guaranteed sugar crash waiting to happen.

Every single month, they showed up at the salon in perfectly matched outfits—*pastel sweater sets, plaid tea-length skirts, nude knee-high stockings that defied weather patterns*—and teal-tinted bouffants that required a level of hair engineering bordering on the architectural.

But that wasn't the worst of it.

No, the worst part was Denice's rare magical allergy to peanuts and tree nuts that triggered *literal fireball sneezing.*

Ask me how I know.

Last time someone brought a peanut butter granola bar into the salon, we had to call in the local fire department—which if it happened now, would include *him*.

Ryan.

My Bear-shaped walking distraction with a firefighter's uniform and a beard that made me consider decisions I'd only make during full moons and ovulation.

But we were *not* thinking about Ryan right now. And we weren't going to do anything that made him appear in all his firefighting glory.

Nope.

Focus, Donny.

Work, not peanut butter cookie substitutions or hot Shifters who make you want to shave your legs daily just in case.

"By the way," Celeste said, dragging me out of my spiral. "You got a letter from the property manager. Something about your lease—Donny? Earth to Donny?"

"Huh?" I blinked.

My brain had wandered off again, probably in the direction of Ryan's biceps.

Celeste narrowed her eyes at me.

"I said you have mail. But you've been staring into space and scratching your head for like, five minutes. You okay?"

"I'm fine," I said, even as my scalp continued to *itch like a cursed jockstrap.*

Celeste tilted her head.

"You sure? Your aura's doing that weird static thing. And your energy spikes every time I say the word *cookie.*"

She smirked.

"Watch the store," I snapped, heading toward the back. "I need to use the potty."

"Donny, wait—*oh my Goddess!*"

That shriek was the kind of noise reserved for breakups, Ghost sightings, and surprise glitter bombs.

"What?" I demanded, freezing mid-step.

"Your hair!"

My hair? Goddess, no!

I bolted to the closest mirror—*conveniently located exactly two feet from my face*—and let out a gasp so loud, a nearby shampoo bottle rolled off the counter in fear.

Because my hair?

Was actually—*oh my shit!*

ON. FORKING. FIRE.

Not metaphorically.

Not in the *you're a smoke show* kind of way.

Literal. Forking. Flames.

Orange-blue sparks danced at my roots, and wisps of smoke curled around my scalp like I was about to ascend to Witch heaven or maybe summon a very fashionable Fire Demon.

My mouth opened and closed.

I blinked. Twice.

And then?

I *let loose*.

A filthy, spell-scorching, soul-cleansing stream of cursing flew from my lips like a verbal exorcism.

My employees ducked for cover.

I saw Gigi drop her flat iron.

Marigold dove behind her chair like we were under magical siege.

And me?

I was too far gone.

"AHHHHHHHH! I'm gonna kill that ASSFACED-MOTHERFUCKING-TREE-HUMP-ING-DICKFACED-BUNGHOLE-GIGGLEBERRY-LICKING-COOTER-SNIFFING-STANKASS-DOUCHE-CANOE-PRICKLESS-ARMPIT-BREATH-HAVING-UNIBROWED-SWEATER-UNRAVELING-FUCKWIT!"

Dead silence followed.

Even the hairdryer stopped whirring.

A Ghost might've moaned in agreement.

Gigi's client, poor Kallie Gold, looked like she was about to clutch her pearls and faint.

Delilah Dolittle whispered, "My stars," and crossed herself, even though she was Pagan.

Celeste's mouth hung open. "Donny," she whispered. "Your hair is, like, sizzling. Oh wow, it's, it's BLONDE!"

Something snorted off in the corner, and I turned my glare to the only creature who could be responsible.

GRYN.

That furry demon in Domovyk form was here. In my salon. After sitting in my sweater nest all damn day, cackling like the little bastard he was, clutching his sides and pointing at the strands of my magically imbued hair like he'd just won some victory.

Oh, he wanted a war?

He just got one.

"YOU LITTLE SHIT!"

"Not shit. Domovyk. Better put that out Witchy, or *Hair Now, Gone Tomorrow* will be the real deal for you!"

He was right. The jerk.

First—I needed water, or a fire extinguisher, or possibly Ryan's number on speed dial.

I dunked my head in the nearest sink, gave it a

good, angry scrub, and flipped it up like I was in a forking shampoo commercial directed by Quentin Tarantino.

Ready to summon fireballs and vengeance, I whirled around, prepared to drag that tiny turd-dropping freak to the fifth layer of magical hell by his tail—but the Domojerk was gone.

Of course he was.

Slippery little bastard probably sensed my rage spike and dimension-hopped into someone else's linen closet.

I barely had time to breathe before CRACK-KABOOM—a bolt of forking pink lightning tore through the ceiling like the wrath of a glitter-obsessed goddess and zapped me square on my sore ass.

"OW! SONOFA—!"

That was as far as I got before Celeste, quick as a caffeinated cat, crammed a cookie in my mouth to save me from another verbal sin—*and another divine zapping.*

I bit down in rage.

Chewed in fury.

Okay, okay.

The cookie was actually decent.

A little dry, but this one was surprisingly peanut-free, so at least no spontaneous combustion from Denice Chicky was in my future.

"It's chocolate," she whispered, answering my unspoken question.

Still. Not. The. Point.

I glared at my receptionist as if I could set her eyebrows on fire with sheer willpower.

And judging by the way her eyes widened, and she zipped her lip, she might've believed it was possible.

The rest of the salon was dead silent.

Gigi and Marigold were crouched behind their styling chairs like I'd turned into a magical landmine.

Their clients, Kallie and Delilah, looked ready to evacuate through the plumbing if necessary.

And that's when the bell above the door jingled.

Because of course it did.

Because, of course, *now* is when he would walk in.

There stood Ryan Forking McLeod.

Decked out in full fireman regalia—*big boots, suspenders, tight shirt clinging to muscles sculpted by the gods of emergency response.*

The man looked like a centerfold for *Hot First*

Responders Who Want to Ruin You in the Best Way Possible.

And he was staring at me like I was his forking dessert.

Could be the way my wet hair had soaked through my blouse, but I'd never know because I wasn't asking.

I gulped so hard, I almost choked on a cookie crumb.

No. Nope. Nuh-uh.

Maybe? But no. Better not.

I was so not going down that road.

Not when Evie was floating around on cloud nine with her mate and Bella had her smugly efficient Domovyk helping her bake award-winning pastries and charm the entire town.

No, thank you.

I had trust issues.

And trauma.

And absolutely zero emotional bandwidth for some giant, brooding, smoke-scented Shifter who could carry me like a bridal bouquet and ruin me with one hand.

Nope. I was keeping things professional.

Even if I could practically smell the maple and bear pheromones radiating off him like sin-flavored cologne.

"Someone said there was a fire?" he asked, his lips twitching as he scanned the room—*and then very purposefully lowered his gaze to my hair, keeping those brown beauties away from my wet shirt.*

"Yeah? Well, it's out," I snapped, crossing my arms tightly to hold my composure, and my boobs, which had decided this was the moment to heave like I was on the cover of a trashy romance novel.

"It's um, *blonde,*" he whispered, seemingly awestruck.

"It's fine!" I snapped. "I can fix this."

I pulled out my phone, flipped the camera, and glared at the back reflection of my suddenly not-brunette self.

With a wave of my fingers, a few golden sparkles, and a wiggle of my nose and my hair dried quick as lightning. I ran my fingers through it and inspected.

Honey blonde.

Ash blonde.

Gold-tipped layers with dimensional waves.

I looked like I'd stepped out of a high-end editorial shoot for *Haunt Couture: The Magical Edition.*

It was phenomenal.

Too phenomenal.

"I will murder him with a rubber spatula," I hissed through my teeth.

"Honestly, Donny," Celeste whispered, trying for damage control. "It looks—*kinda amazing.*"

I zapped a warning spark out of my fingertips, and she shut up like a good little receptionist-in-training.

Ryan was still staring at me.

That same weird, soft look on his face, like I was the last donut in the box and he was on a low-carb diet.

I didn't like it.

Well, I did, but I refused to acknowledge it.

"Thank you, but the fire is out. And you can tell your pal Petyr to tell his pal Gryn," I growled, stabbing a finger in the air, "that his days are numbered. Numbered!"

Thunder cracked in the sky.

Everyone froze.

I held my pose, then slowly dropped my hand.

"See? Even the weather's on my side."

Ryan blinked. "I think that was an airplane landing at the municipal airport—"

"Shut it, Smokey. I'm on a roll."

And with that dramatic exit line, I pivoted on my heeled boots, stormed to the back of the salon, and left a trail of tension, judgment, and chocolate cookie crumbs in my wake.

I didn't have any more coffee.

I didn't have any more snacks.

My scalp still tingled from all the fire, and my ass was sore from the Goddess' lightning. Plus, my thighs were clenched so hard whenever he was around, I very seriously regretted every missed yoga class.

But I had a job to do.

Hair to style.

Witches to appease.

And a three-foot demonic furball to destroy.

Blonde or not, I was gonna survive the day.

You're darn tootin'!

CHAPTER FOURTEEN-DONNY

I HAD a break between appointments and was just finishing my second attempt to reverse the hair-hex that Domoprick cast on me when the door slammed open hard enough to jingle the wards.

"OMG! Celeste was telling the truth?" Evie screeched, bursting into the salon like a one-woman parade. "You went full Marilyn on us without even showing me first?"

She stomped in, hours early for her highlights appointment, brown curls bouncing, oversized sunglasses perched dramatically on her head like she was channeling her inner Norma Desmond.

"You're early," Celeste noted helpfully, still chewing that awful gum she thought made her look cool.

"I know, but I'm the mayor. My schedule is chaos incarnate. Donny understands. Right, Donny?"

I lifted my head slowly, like something ancient and angry rising from a cursed crypt.

If she reached for my hair, I was going to bite her. Or possibly cry. The jury was still out.

"But wowza, I was not prepared for this," Evie breathed, hands flailing like she was a car lot air dancer come to life.

Don't drop the dye, Donny. Do not drop the dye on your blouse.

Celeste, ever the announcer of the obvious, piped up with a dramatic sigh.

"Donatella hasn't said a word since this went down."

Evie didn't care. She was already across the black-and-white tile floor in two Witchy strides, hip-checking a waiting room chair out of her way like a pro.

I stayed silent. Not because I didn't have things to say. Oh, I had plenty.

But they were mostly murder threats directed at a certain furry goblin who'd bleach-bombed my iconic tresses.

There are three things sacred to Donatella Andrews:

1. Her coffee.

2. Her clothes.

3. Her hair.

And Gryn had dared to mess with number three.

My nose twitched—*literally*—and a perfectly timed poof of sink water splashed Evie right in the nose just as she tried to touch one of the still-foiled strands of my redemption dye job.

"Rude," she said, dabbing her nose with the sleeve of her very-expensive-for-someone-who-never-leaves-town sweater. "I'm just not used to seeing you so, so *California*."

Even Celeste had dropped her jaw when I came in this morning with Gryn's unsolicited golden glow-up.

Like I was some kind of reject from a magical Malibu Barbie prototype.

"Well, I would've said keep it," Evie declared, plopping into the chair beside me with all the subtlety of a rhinoceros in a tutu.

"We could've gone with my idea for the Halloween Bash theme!"

Celeste, who I had trained well, appeared like magic, which she probably actually used this time, with a tray of foils, a mixing bowl, clips, and the bleach I'd be applying the correct way.

For Evie. Not for me.

I was back to brunette again, thank you very much.

"I mean, think about it—me as Jean Harlow. Bella as Jayne Mansfield. The girl's got the hooters for it. And you, Donny, could've been Marilyn."

I rolled my eyes so hard I swear I saw last week.

Evie was grinning now, eyes all twinkly with evil excitement.

"Come on, you in that white dress from The Seven Year Itch? Hot damn."

"She'd kill it," Celeste chimed in unhelpfully from the corner.

"Yeah," I muttered, setting my jaw. "Me. Marilyn? Ha. I'm more Bettie Page. Me as Monroe? Hmph. My round ass."

Evie didn't blink.

"Bettie was hotter than sin, and you know it. And Monroe? That woman had curves for days. She'd have been a full-on Instagram baddie today."

Celeste, gods help her, decided to speak.

"Actually, she'd be considered plus sized by modern standards," she said innocently.

And that was it.

You could feel the magic pressure in the room spike like a barometer on a hurricane watch.

"EXCUSE me?" Evie barked, rounding on her like a wrathful sorority president.

"I mean—I didn't mean it like that—" Celeste sputtered.

Evie stood, fists planted on her hips, fingers sparking. "Listen here, Infant. This is what's wrong with the internet. You think a size four is plus-sized because of whatever bullcrap filters are pumped into those body apps on VampTok."

I sighed and backed away slowly from the dye station. It was about to get real.

"Marilyn Monroe had a 24-inch waist. Twenty. Four. And curves. And class. And she didn't take sass from some wild-haired baby Witch who doesn't know shit about fuck!"

Celeste shrank behind the reception desk, face pale, gum forgotten.

Pink lightning danced across the ceiling, but for some reason no one got zapped.

I almost felt bad.

Almost.

Evie spun back toward me like a fury on espresso.

"Donny, you'd make a kickass Marilyn. Admit it. Just say yes. Halloween Bash. Bombshell theme. Let's do it."

"No," I said, yanking my towel turban off my head and flicking my fingers to dry my hair.

Rich, dark brunette locks fell in waves down my back.

The familiar weight of them grounded me like a magical security blanket.

The golden locks were gone. Order had been restored.

But, well, I didn't feel quite as relieved as I'd expected.

Something about the blonde had made me feel bold.

Reckless.

Just a little unhinged in the best way.

And maybe I needed a little unhinged in my life.

Still. No one messed with Donatella Andrews' hair. Except Donatella Andrews.

I really have got to stop thinking about myself in third person.

"You know," Evie mused, watching me style with narrowed eyes. "It is weird that Gryn targeted your hair."

"It's not my weakness," I grumbled, reaching for my big round brush.

"You sure about that?" she teased. "He could've hexed your Prada boots. Your Gucci slacks."

"If he even laid a paw on my boots, I'd bury him in a backyard full of soul-sucking mushrooms," I muttered.

"Okay, okay. But maybe—*and just hear me out*—maybe he's not trying to ruin your life."

I gave her a look so flat it could've been pressed between dictionary pages.

"I said maybe."

I pointed the blow dryer at her and gave it a blast.

"Fine!" she laughed. "Don't listen to your glorious, wise, fashionable bestie."

"I'm not listening," I muttered.

Evie just grinned.

Celeste slowly peeked out from behind the desk, eyes wide, lips zipped.

Smart girl.

And me?

I had no idea what Gryn was planning. Or why he decided to turn me into a magical blonde bombshell. But I knew one thing for sure.

Payback was coming. And it was gonna be fabulous. But that had to wait.

I grunted and winced, dragging the round brush through my hair like it was possessed—which, given the week I was having, wasn't entirely off the table.

"Ow. Forking hell," I muttered, tugging at another stubborn knot.

The strands were smooth and shiny but tangled like a conspiracy.

Probably the combination of two chemical treatments, a gallon of magical interference, and enough emotional trauma to qualify as a *Telenovela* subplot.

Still, I was feeling smug.

Victorious, even.

I had beaten Gryn.

My hair was espresso brown again, glossy and rich, like the coffee I'd inhaled ten minutes ago.

Balance had been restored.

My crown reclaimed.

Turning slightly, I looked over at Evie, who was in the chair beside mine attempting to brush out her own hair like she was reenacting a scene from a horror movie.

She'd somehow managed to create a bird's nest at the nape of her neck, and I was debating whether to intervene or just let her learn from her mistakes.

Despite the hair carnage, I admired her outfit.

Burnt-orange pencil pants, a high-neck blouse buttoned all the way to her chin, and a brooch that screamed I brunch with Aunt Bea from Mayberry.

She was straight out of Bewitched, and she loved it.

Evie's whole aesthetic was mid-century magical housewife. Meanwhile, I lived and died by whatever haute couture label was brave enough to cut clothes for women with actual asses.

It wasn't easy to find designer pieces that loved me back, but thankfully my magic had taste. A little charm here, a bit of tailoring there, and boom—my closet was a temple to stretchy couture.

Fashion was my happy place.

Magic was my job.

Hair was my art.

But lately, things were off.

Like, dangerously off.

I could feel it under my skin, jittering like static. Something inside was teetering. I didn't like it.

"Uh, Donny?" Evie's voice cut through my spiral.

I was halfway through mixing the bleach for her highlights and not really in the mood for another detour.

"What?" I asked, not looking up.

"You, um, might want to turn around."

"Nope."

Evie narrowed her eyes.

"Don't be a child. Turn around."

"I don't think so."

I dropped the brush on my station and rubbed my now-sweaty palms on my navy pinstriped slacks.

They were Gucci.

I adored them.

Wide-legged perfection, soft as sin, with just enough tailoring to make my waist look snatched and my butt look like a snack.

Paired with a cream silk blouse? I was thriving.

Until I wasn't.

My clothes were among the few things still in my control.

Unlike my traitorous follicles, which I'd feared had decided they liked being blonde.

"Donny! Just look in the mirror!"

With a heavy sigh and a healthy dose of dread, I turned.

"What the actual fork!?" I gasped.

My hair—*my blessed, brown, espresso perfection*—was already lightening. Again.

Not even being subtle about it.

Gold shimmered through the strands like sunlight mocking me.

"AHHHHHHHHH!" I screamed, flailing with all the drama of a soap opera villainess who'd just been slapped.

"Oh, honey," Evie murmured, rushing to my side like I was a wounded puppy.

"I'm gonna kill that furry-assed, tail-having, horn-wearing Domodick!" I shrieked, shaking a fist at the ceiling like the Goddess herself might back me up.

No lightning.

No smiting.

Huh.

Maybe she was letting that one slide.

Bless her.

I plopped into the nearest empty salon chair and buried my face in my hands.

This was war.

"Donny?" Celeste's voice was soft, tentative. "I brought your coffee and croissant. Bella called. Said you might need it."

My heart twisted.

I hadn't even noticed she was gone. And now here she was, being sweet and thoughtful, after I'd practically bit her head off earlier.

What the hell was wrong with me?

"See?" Evie said. "Even Celeste gets you. You're just hangry and cursed. Happens to the best of us."

"I don't get it," I groaned, taking the croissant like

it was a life raft. "Gryn hates me. And I don't even know why."

"He doesn't hate you," Celeste offered as I chomped into the pastry.

Evie raised a brow at her. "Shh. Not helping."

"Mmmm," I moaned, eyes fluttering closed.

The croissant was warm, flaky, buttery heaven.

"Okay, but—*seriously*—did Bella put something new in these?" I asked, licking a rogue crumb off my lip.

"Actually," Evie said, too casually. "Jaxson told me Ryan's been exclusively baking all the complicated layery stuff lately."

I froze. Mid-chew.

My Bear Shifter baker crush made this?

My traitorous tastebuds started humming a mating song. I narrowed my eyes and aimed my brush at Evie's head like a wand.

She yelped when I yanked a little too hard.

"Oops."

"Liar," she muttered, rubbing her scalp.

"What? Maybe he just knows your taste," Celeste piped up from the front desk. "Your familiar. Not the baker Bear. Well, actually, I mean, maybe Ryan does, too."

"Still not helping, Celeste," Evie and I said in unison.

"Sorry," she whispered.

I stood up, brushing pastry crumbs from my lap and shaking out my ridiculous, cursed, slowly re-blonding mane.

Whatever was going on between me and Gryn—*and me and Ryan*—I needed to get it together.

There were roots to touch up and Witches to bleach.

And if anyone else suggested I looked good blonde, I was gonna start hexing.

CHAPTER FIFTEEN-RYAN

I'D NEVER BEEN this twitchy about a damn haircut before.

Pacing in the locker room of the Castor's Corner Firehouse, I pulled at the collar of my cleanest Henley for the tenth time.

I'd already changed shirts twice.

Tried the navy one, then the black.

Settled on the charcoal gray because it brought out my eyes—or so Bella claimed.

Not that I was trying to impress anyone.

Bullshit. I was trying to impress *her*.

Donny freaking Andrews.

The curvy Witch who'd invaded every waking thought since the first time I stepped into her salon and got a whiff of her vanilla-honey-magical hell scent.

She was fire.

Fury. Flawless.

And I was so screwed.

"Dude," Conrad called from the kitchen, "you wearing cologne or marinating in it?"

I growled. "Shut up."

He poked his head around the corner, raised a brow at the five empty coffee cups stacked next to me.

"You alright?"

"I'm getting my hair cut."

He blinked slowly. "Okaaayyyy. Are you dying or what?"

"It's *her*," I muttered, pacing again. "Donny."

"Ohhh," he drawled, coming fully into view and leaning against the wall like he was about to enjoy a damn soap opera. "So, today is the day."

"Yep. Today is it," I grunted, dragging a hand through my shaggy curls. "I asked to come in early. But she's booked till tonight. I got the last appointment of the day."

"Sounds like fate."

"It's a haircut."

"It's a *mating ritual,*" he countered. "Did you exfoliate?"

"What? No! I—what?"

How did he?

I paused. No sense in lying. Shifters could tell about that sort of thing.

"Maybe."

Conrad cackled. I considered throwing my boots at him.

"I just want to make an impression. She always looks so good, and she smells *too* good," I said, barely getting the words out without groaning.

"Yeah?"

"Oh yeah. Like honey and sin, and expensive shampoo. And she talks with her hands. Long fingers. Soft skin. I want her hands all over—"

"And there it is. TMI, bro," Conrad winced and reached for his phone. "Do I need to get Jaxson on the line to talk you down?"

I ignored him. My whole body buzzed with energy. I was too hot.

My Bear stirred under my skin, restless.

I had a couple of hours before I needed to get to Hair Now, Gone Tomorrow.

I had no idea what to do with myself in the meantime.

"Okay, calm down," I said out loud, adjusting my shirt one more time. "You're just going in for a haircut. She's going to touch your head for twenty-five, maybe thirty minutes tops. You are a man. You are composed. You are not going to Shift—"

CRACK.

The back door of the firehouse exploded.

I looked down at my paws.

Oh. Shit.

I'd Shifted.

Full-on Grizzly.

"Bro," Conrad said from behind the shattered remnants of the door. "That was mahogany."

I snorted and stomped the ground, ears twitching.

"Better run off some of that energy before you show up drooling on her salon floor," he advised, already grabbing tools. "Don't worry. I'll fix the door."

I huffed out a breath, nodded once, and lumbered off into the woods behind the firehouse, the lingering scent of honey and hair dye already taunting my poor lovesick Bear.

I was doomed.

CHAPTER SIXTEEN-DONNY

STYLISTS WERE like bartenders in the sense that people tended to treat their appointments like pseudo-therapy sessions.

I was used to it.

And sometimes I even enjoyed it.

But as my bestie turned cousin rambled on about her change in relationship status from woefully single to happily mated, I found myself growing oddly depressed.

Not only was she blissfully getting boinked every night—but Evie was suddenly on my case about my lack of said boinking.

But just because Evie was getting hot and heavy with a certain smexy Wolf Shifter didn't mean the rest of us needed to hop on the supernatural sausage train.

"Evie, I am not into the Bear. Period."

"Yeah, right," she muttered.

"I'm not!"

But whether I was trying to convince her or myself it didn't matter.

That was my story, and I was sticking to it.

The Bear was not for me.

No matter how good his pastries were.

"Come on, Evie, I thought we agreed not to talk about him," I growled, setting the bleach bowl down a little harder than necessary.

"You can't run from your fate," she sing-songed. "Besides, looks like you need a good boinkfest."

My girly bits bristled in betrayal.

I didn't need my BFF rubbing salt—*and lust*—in the wound.

"Evie," I warned, lifting the brush coated in enough bleach to strip the paint off a car. "Unless you want me to lighten your eyebrows down to invisible, I suggest you shaddap. It's not fair of you to rub your suddenly overactive sex life in my face."

She snorted. Loudly. The beyotch. She was lucky I loved her like a sister.

I went back to sectioning off her hair, smearing the magic-infused bleach with practiced strokes.

Highlighting was a sacred art form, and I was determined to make her look like a pinup angel no matter how annoying she was being.

"I'm just saying there's no shame in it, Donny," she said innocently, "besides, no one thinks you're gonna boink the Bear just because he bakes."

"Who's boinking woodland creatures?!" Celeste gasped, dropping the mail all over the salon floor like she'd just heard someone hex a kitten.

"Celeste!" I barked. "Put the mail away, go back to your desk, and answer the crapping phone like I pay you to."

"But—"

"The only butt you need to worry about is your own, and it better be in that chair before I zap it into next week."

Celeste squeaked and scrambled.

Not fast enough.

I sent a little magical zap! right into her backside.

Nothing dangerous. Just enough sting to make her hop.

"OW! This is so wrong!"

"Then quit!" I snapped.

For the record, she wouldn't.

She never did. I wasn't even sure how I'd hired her in the first place.

She just showed up one day.

Like a caffeinated mirage with bubble gum and zero boundaries.

"You angry 'cause your birthday's coming up?" Celeste called from behind the register.

Snarl. Snort. Zap.

She yelped again. Good. That's what she got for poking the Witch.

Fifteen minutes later, the salon was finally quiet.

Evie sat flipping through a vintage fashion mag.

I'd finished her highlights in record time and worked off my rage with some magically boosted hair perfection.

"Evie," I said, my tone sweet as spun sugar. "Don't you have something better to do than harass me all afternoon? You are the mayor."

"Yes, I am," she said primly. "And today, I'm playing hooky."

My brows rose. "Oh, are you now?"

"Mm hmm." She stood and twirled like a 1960s Barbie, admiring her reflection. "I have a date."

A zip of satisfaction tingled up my spine. Her highlights looked amazing. Perfectly toned. Just enough shimmer to make her glow.

"Shame on you, Madame Mayor," I teased, folding my arms. "Abandoning your post for a man."

"As if. Stanley's got it covered." She tossed her hair. "Besides, it's a picnic down by the falls."

Celeste's head popped up like a prairie dog. "Aren't the falls closed?"

Evie smiled sweetly. "Yes, Celeste. That's why I, the mayor, can still go. Duh."

"She's gonna get ticks on her butt," I muttered.

"Ugh! Don't say that!" Evie swatted at her pants like one had already latched on.

Snicker.

I couldn't help myself.

Then it happened.

A low rumble echoed outside the salon—deep and sexy.

My stomach did a ridiculous little flip. But of course, this rumble was not mine.

I turned just in time to see Evie's Wolf Shifter mate pull up on his Harley, wind in his thick black hair, leather jacket tight across his chest like some forbidden biker dream.

Evie glowed.

No, seriously.

Aqua and silver sparks flickered across her body,

a soft swirl of magic that shimmered like moonlight on a lake.

It was all very fated-matey.

I rolled my eyes so hard I nearly gave myself a migraine.

"Wow, she's literally lighting up," Celeste whispered.

Evie's smile was pure joy as she rushed to the door.

Jaxson stood there, tall and annoyingly hot, eyes locked on her like no one else existed.

"Donny," he said with a nod, but his voice was pure velvet for Evie.

I crossed my arms and squinted. "Okay, love-birds. Children present."

"I am not a child!" Celeste shouted.

"Bye, Donny! See ya, Celeste!" Evie called, waving as she skipped out the door like a teenage girl with her first crush.

"Don't get a tick on your butt!" I yelled after her.

"Don't think I won't zap you for that later!" she called back.

I grinned. "Bring it, mayor."

"You know," Evie had shouted, wrapping her arms around her man, "you look good as a blonde!"

I blinked. Wiggled my fingers.

"Don't think I won't get you back, Evie Castor!" I yelled out the door, but I knew she'd be gone before I could retaliate.

Jaxson revved the engine like a thunder god, then they roared off toward their romantic waterfall picnic.

Lucky forkers.

Once again, silence fell inside the salon, but it was short-lived.

I barely had time to sigh.

The bell jingled again, and I turned just in time to see my next clients arrive—a trio of Cat Shifter sisters who smelled like baby powder and floral perfume.

Great.

Another day, another round of magical mayhem and high-end hair.

But one thing was certain.

The blonde was not staying.

Probably.

Maybe.

Ugh.

Where the fork was my espresso?

CHAPTER SEVENTEEN-DONNY

"WELL, WHAT HAVE WE HERE?"

The hair on the back of my neck stood up like a static-charged wool sweater as two of my most ornery clients strutted into *Hair Now, Gone Tomorrow* like they owned the joint.

The Chickie twins.

Saints preserve us.

Now, on a normal day, these two were a cauldron of cranky in matching orthopedic shoes.

But today? Oh, I could already tell.

Today, they'd arrived with a purpose.

And that purpose was to ruin mine.

They wore their usual ensembles—shapeless, violet, tea-length dresses that somehow made them look simultaneously washed-out and radioactive.

Add in knee-highs that were exactly two shades darker than their winter-parchment skin and sensible beige shoes from the ninth circle of fashion hell, and boom.

Fashion crime scene.

I touched two fingers to my temples and rubbed in slow, calming circles.

Breathe, Donny.

Inhale, exhale.

They may look like elderly grape-colored throw pillows, but they were still high-ranking Witches in our community.

And while I might be a badass stylist with a flair for flair, I wasn't looking to get hexed into a toad for serving attitude.

The thing was, lately they'd stopped hiding their age.

That meant they were getting ready to move on —to the Next Amazing Journey or their next magical phase, whatever that was.

Either reincarnation or retirement in some heavenly version of Boca. Who knew?

But seeing them like this—flesh sagging, wrinkles unapologetically flaunted—was a reminder that I, too, had an expiration date.

I might be magical, but I wasn't immortal.

My birthday loomed like a vulture on a sugar detox, and the idea of getting older was starting to itch under my skin like a poorly placed lace thong.

Still, I pasted on a smile that could rival Miss America.

"You know, dear, blonde is a nice—" Denice began.

"—look on you," Candice finished for her, per usual.

"But we do not approve—"

"—of eating in the shop."

Their gazes landed on the coffee-stained napkin and flaky croissant crumbs littering my sleek waiting area like I'd been running a damn *Bed & Breakfast* instead of a salon.

I flushed.

"Oh! That's mine! So sorry, ladies," Celeste chimed in brightly.

Bless her. My assistant—*part-time receptionist, full-time chaos half-Goblin*—swooped in like a blue-haired Valkyrie and started scooping up the mess.

I blinked at her in confusion. She *never* took the blame for anything. Like, ever.

"Hmmph," Denice grumbled, watching Celeste with a glare that could sour milk.

"I don't know, DeDe. I liked her better as a

brunette," Candice whispered, still staring directly at me like I was a zoo exhibit.

"Excuse me," Celeste said again, darting in front of me as she gathered up the garbage.

It was then that I caught her wide eyes and a flash of true panic.

Look down, she mouthed.

I did.

Oh forking fudge.

My hands were glowing gold.

Not cute shimmer glow.

Not spa-day sparkle glow.

Nope. This was full-on *you're-about-to-explode-with-witch-rage* glow.

I was seconds away from reducing the Chickie twins to smoldering piles of orthopedic ash.

With a squeak, I turned to the sink and stuck my hands under cold water like I was prepping for surgery.

Goddess take the wheel.

My magic was out of control.

AGAIN.

Celeste, the beautiful, annoying, slightly feral creature, kept her cool. She made a million apologies, bowed like she was in a Jane Austen novel, and even offered to get the twins fresh tea.

Tea!

Like we served that here, for fork's sake.

I owed her a raise. I also owed her an apology. I would do neither, of course. But I'd think about it while I faked washing my hands.

Once the glowing faded and I was back in control, I took a moment to assess the damage.

My reflection stared back at me.

I was a stranger.

But maybe, just maybe, I was more myself now than I've ever been before.

And that shook me to the core.

Honey blonde locks. Shimmery. Shiny. Possibly even beautiful.

The Domodouchebag had done *too good* a job, the smug little familiar freak.

Plus, his spell proved impenetrable, and my natural brunette glory was nowhere in sight.

Forcing a smile, I turned back to my favorite pain-in-the-asses.

Time to get to work.

"Well, maybe she'll do it right this time," Candice whispered to her sister.

"Doubtful," DeDe replied.

Hours later.

Hair dye was still washing down the drain, the

curlers had been set with precision, and the industrial-strength hair spray was still about, making the air taste like regret and lilacs.

But I did it. I got through it.

No magical explosions.

No combusting biddies.

No bleach mishaps.

Hair Now, Gone Tomorrow didn't smell like your average mortal salon.

No ammonia or acetone disasters here. Nope.

We had standards.

And a magical crematorium in the back.

All organic, eco-friendly, and highly flammable.

See, Witches like me were bound by sacred hairdressing oaths.

You don't mess with a client's free will.

You don't enchant a blowout to last six months.

You definitely don't sneak a glamour spell into a pixie cut without consent.

So, like always, I renewed my vow.

I stepped into the center of the salon, took a deep breath, and whispered the sacred words under my breath:

"Goddess on high,

We pledge to thee,

Maker of all things, beautifully,

To tend the creatures big and small,
To cut their hair, nails, beards, even balls,
Our craft is sacred, we owe to thee,
Our talents without duplicity.
Never to use our patron's prize,
To do magic or harm or change their lives.
To serve magic, our only goal,
To bring others joy tenfold.
As you will, so mote it be."

My magic hummed in agreement, soft and sweet like the purr of a happy kitten.

I grinned.

Even when my hair was blonde and my day was trash, the Goddess still had my back. And that was a good thing.

Witch's honor.

CHAPTER EIGHTEEN-DONNY

SO, magic has rules.

We all know that.

And if I even thought of breaking the sacred code of salon sorcery, the Goddess would flay the magic from my soul and leave my behind rawer than a fresh wax job in July.

And that wasn't even the worst of it.

The last poor Witch who'd betrayed her oath? She didn't just lose her powers—she was cursed to live out her remaining human days with the most abominable hairstyle known to supernatural society.

Yep, you guessed it.

A business-in-the-front, party-in-the-back, wavy-haired mullet with frosted forking tips, which for some reason was making a comeback amongst the younger normals.

Blech.

I shivered at the memory of that cautionary tale. The woman had been excommunicated and ex-hair-styled.

A fate worse than death, in my humble opinion.

Swallowing back my horror, I focused on finishing my duties before my last clients arrived.

I gathered all the stray clippings from the day—*snippets of hair, shards of nail, and magical residue*—and funneled them into the enchanted tube system that led to the in-house crematorium, where they would be purified in accordance with the Covenant of Salon Sorcery.

Hair Now, Gone Tomorrow didn't play around.

We might be cozy and Witchy and covered in pink glitter, but we followed the Goddess' rules to the letter.

As I sealed the last tube with a satisfying pop, I heard Celeste's voice behind me.

"You sure you don't want me to stay?"

Ugh. That was the fifth time she'd asked.

I turned just in time to see her sneak a peek at her phone again. I rolled my eyes so hard I might've dislocated a retina. The girl was more obvious than a hexed love potion.

"Of course not. Go on. Shoo. Be gone. Fly free," I said, flapping a hand toward the door.

"But I could cancel my date—"

"Celeste," I cut her off with a pointed look. "You finally got asked out by your dreamboat. You're not canceling. Not after making me eat the same lunch for a month straight just to get a glimpse of his biceps."

Her cheeks flushed. "How did you know I've been crushing on him?"

"Please. I've got better intuition than a Ouija board on a full moon. And I'm starting to look like a dumpling with how much you've made me eat from *Wrap & Roll*. Now, git."

I waved my broom at her for good measure. It worked.

She squeaked and bolted out the door with a mumbled "thank you," nearly tripping over her own feet.

Finally. Peace.

I took a slow, luxurious sip of my lavender-citrus tea, leaning against the counter as the cool fall breeze filtered in through the open window.

Outside, the sun was setting, and the leaves were a riot of color—reds and golds and burnt oranges that made me want to buy fuzzy socks and threaten anyone who spoke ill of pumpkin spice.

It was my season.

Autumn was my vibe.

Witchy and wistful and just a little bit dramatic.

I sighed with contentment, letting the warm mug soothe my hands and my nerves.

And then, a growl.

Not a menacing one, but deep.

Rumbling.

And so forking male it made my knees buckle.

I nearly *yeeted* my mug at the ceiling, but before it could even slip from my fingers, a huge hand caught it mid-air.

"You almost dropped this," said Ryan McLeod in a voice that made my ovaries weep with need.

Sweet sizzling spellcraft, he was close.

Too close.

Not close enough.

And, oh my Goddess, he smelled like smoke and sugar and danger.

"Hey, Donny."

I swallowed hard.

"You scared me."

"My apologies, Honey. I'd never intend to frighten you," he said with a voice so smooth it should be illegal.

I narrowed my eyes to keep from swooning.

He was stupidly tall.

Broad like a fridge.

Hairy like a lumberjack in a shampoo commercial.

His beard was an overgrown mess of auburn and chestnut, and his hair was currently in what I could only assume was a chaotic bun held together by willpower and lies.

Hot? Yes.

But the man needed help. Help only I could deliver.

"Come on," I said, breezing past him, my hair swinging behind me like a gold battle flag. "Let's get you cleaned up."

He followed, silent as a shadow, and lowered himself into the shampoo chair like some kind of mythical beast going into hibernation.

Graceful and deadly.

I pretended not to notice how his gaze tracked me like I was prey. Sexy prey.

Ugh. Get a grip, Donny.

I focused on the basics—*adjust the chair, wet the hair, try not to drool.*

"So," I said, gathering shampoo in my hand. "What exactly do you want me to do?"

He tilted his head, his eyes crinkling at the corners.

"Are we talking about my hair, Honey?"

I paused, realizing I'd stepped right into that one. "Yes. Your hair. And your beard. That's what I'm talking about."

Who was I trying to convince? Him or me?

"Whatever you say, Honey."

Ermagerd. Honey. HONEY?!

It just dawned on me he was a Bear. And Bears liked honey.

Specifically, they liked to eat it.

I bit my lip hard enough to make my eyes water.

This was getting ridiculous. I was a professional. A licensed magical stylist with wards on her scissors and a mini altar in the back room.

I was not going to melt over some rugged Bear Shifter, no matter how good he smelled or how flirty he got.

"Well?" I snapped, trying for impatient instead of flustered.

He shrugged. "Didn't really have a plan. I trust you."

I blinked. "*You* trust *me*?"

"Yep. Go on. Do whatever you want. I know I'm in good hands."

Sweet forking stardust.

That was the sexiest sentence I'd ever heard.

And it wasn't even dirty.

I turned away to hide my blush and turned the water on with a flick of my wrist.

Adjusting the temperature, I began working the shampoo into his hair.

He groaned.

I pretended not to hear it.

Focus, Donny. Focus.

His hair was—*surprisingly*—glorious.

Not coarse like I expected.

Just thick. Soft. Like brushed velvet with streaks of silver and gold glinting under the light.

The silver made me think. How old was he? Did Shifters age like Witches? Suddenly, I was full of questions, but I didn't dare ask them.

Focus on the hair, Donny.

I rinsed and conditioned. Then, I did the same to the beard on his face.

It wasn't much different from the hair on his head.

Wild, yes, but underneath the chaos was luxury.

The man was a walking ad for conditioner.

"I'm forty-seven, by the way," he said out of nowhere.

I startled.

"What?"

"You were wondering how old I was," he said, one brow raised, that same wicked little smirk dancing across his lips. "I could hear it. Sorry. It's a thing."

Holy. Forking. Hell.

Mind reading. *Forking mind reading.*

That was a mate thing.

A fated mates thing.

I was going to die right here.

Buried alive under a mountain of pheromones and panic.

"What's on your mind, Donatella? I can practically hear your wheels turning. Come on. Talk to me, Honey."

That did it.

I slapped a dollop of conditioner on his forehead.

"Ow!" he laughed.

I smiled wickedly.

"Oops. My bad."

"Do I need to worry?" he asked, mock-serious. "Should I prepare myself for a mohawk?"

"Depends. You planning to flirt with me all night or let me do my job?"

"Can't it be both?"

This Bear was going to be the death of me.

But oh, what a beautiful death it would be.

CHAPTER NINETEEN-RYAN

I WAS VIBRATING WITH ANTICIPATION.

Not just a little jittery.

Not a bit of nervous energy.

Full-body, bone-deep, animal-on-the-edge vibrating.

I'd barely slept all week, too keyed up thinking about her. Donny Andrews. The Witch. The woman who haunted my dreams and tied my Bear up in knots with a single glance.

And now? I was finally going to feel her hands on me.

Not the way I wanted—*yet*—but I'd take what I could get.

A haircut. That's all this was supposed to be.

So why the hell did I feel like I was about to walk

into a claiming ceremony?

I pulled up to Hair Now, Gone Tomorrow, my jeans sticking a little too tight to my thighs because someone had baked three trays of cinnamon knots at 3AM to burn off tension.

Someone with paws.

Someone with feelings.

Someone who'd ripped the firehouse back door off its hinges earlier today because the idea of this haircut had me so wired I accidentally Shifted when I caught her scent on the breeze.

"*Better run off some of that energy, bro,*" Conrad had said. "*No worries, I'll fix the door.*"

Yeah. Sure.

Fat lot of good that did.

Now I was here. At her salon.

Standing just outside the front door, doing deep breathing like a damn yoga Bear and trying not to embarrass myself by knocking over a newspaper stand with my tail.

I inhaled.

Donny's scent hit me like a sucker punch to the solar plexus—wildflower honey and vanilla and magic—and beneath it, *need.*

Her need.

It curled around me like silk and fire. I could scent her magic on the air—*agitated, spicy, flirtatious.*

Her desire was pulsing through this place like it had soaked into the floors and mirrors.

She was aroused. Whether she admitted it or not.

She wanted me.

And my Bear? The beast was roaring with approval.

I pushed open the door, and her voice hit me first.

Sharp, exasperated, full of sass.

Goddess, I could listen to her yell at her assistant all day.

Then I saw her.

My Donny.

She was wearing something different now. But that made sense since before she'd been soaked.

Honestly, if I had to think about her walking around all day in wet clothes, I'd lose my mind.

Right now she had on black leggings, a smock with paint splatter-like streaks of pastel magic across the chest, and her new honey blonde hair was floating behind her like a flag waving in the wind before a battle.

Her cheeks were flushed, magic glittering gold on her fingertips.

Her hips swayed even when she wasn't moving.

Her lips were pursed in concentration.

She was chaos.

Beauty.

Fire and honey—*my Honey*—all rolled into one bite-sized Witch bomb.

And she smelled like she missed me.

Not that she'd say that.

Not that I'd push for that admission.

Not yet anyway.

"Hey, Donny," I said, my voice a little too deep, a little too rough.

Her eyes met mine, and something flared there—surprise, hesitation, then heat.

She recovered fast though, waving me toward the chair like I was just another walk-in off the street and not her fated mate.

But she knew it. Deep down in her Witchy soul she fucking knew exactly who I was to her.

Some banter and the sexiest shampoo session later, she was nudging me to a different chair.

Lumbering oaf that I was, it took me a minute. But can you blame me? I mean, she was *so close*.

"Let's go, Smokey the Bear. Sit down right here," she said, like she hadn't been thinking dirty thoughts about me two seconds ago.

I obeyed. Mostly because I'd follow that voice anywhere.

She spun the chair, so I was facing away from the mirror, and ran her fingers through my too long hair.

I exhaled through my nose and resisted the urge to grab her wrist and kiss her palm.

She didn't know how much that touch meant to me.

How hard I'd waited to feel it.

Then she lifted a lock and snipped.

A slow grin spread across my face.

Nice try, sweetheart.

"You trying to scare me?" I asked, glancing up. "Because it's not gonna work. I already said I trust you."

Her fingers stilled for half a second. Then resumed.

"Oh, so you asked around about me?" she shot back, trying for casual, but I heard the hitch in her breath.

"Maybe I did," I murmured. "Why? You care what I do?"

She didn't answer. Not with words.

Just pressed closer, like it was an accident.

Like she didn't realize her hip was nestled

between my thighs.

Like she didn't feel the way I throbbed for her.

Like she wasn't deliberately brushing her body against mine with every pass of the scissors.

My Bear rumbled.

Not loud.

Not threatening.

Just there—a low, constant sound that said, *she's ours*.

That said mine.

That said, *don't fuck this up*.

And she, she was sniffing me.

The moment her nose brushed my neck, I nearly lost it.

I had to close my eyes.

Had to dig my claws into the chair's armrests— not physically, but in my mind.

Because if I touched her now, I'd be begging.

Dropping to my knees in front of her and offering everything I was.

Instead, I stayed still.

Let her sniff me like I was her own personal cinnamon-scented sex candle.

And gods, the way her breath caught?

It was the best damned moment of my life.

She moved between my legs like it was natural.

I held her waist and didn't move a single inch more.

She needed to come to me.

To choose me.

And every second her magic brushed mine?

Every time her fingers trailed through my hair?

It chipped away at my restraint.

I let her trim and buzz and tease.

I let her run her fingers over my scalp and tug gently.

I let her get as close as she wanted, because I was done hiding what I felt.

My arousal was thick in the air now.

My Shifter scent wrapped around her like a cocoon.

I didn't force it.

I didn't push.

I simply let her feel it.

Let her decide if she wanted to breathe me in.

And the way her lips parted? The way her breathing hitched? The way her thighs pressed tighter?

She wanted to.

Oh, I fucking knew she wanted me.

And it was the single hottest moment of my life.

By the time she reached for the razor, I was half feral.

Her touch was reverent, careful, slow.

She shaved me with the same grace a priestess might use to tend to a sacred blade.

When she whispered beautiful—*thinking I didn't hear*—I almost dropped the mask.

"You have no idea," I replied, voice raw.

Her gaze clashed with mine, and it was full of confusion, hope, longing, lust.

She was already mine.

She just didn't know it yet.

So I waited. I stayed still. I didn't rush in like I wanted to—*was desperate to*.

"It's your choice, Honey," I whispered when she finally raised her big, beautiful eyes to mine.

Because when Donatella Andrews finally fell into my arms? I wasn't letting go.

Mine.

CHAPTER TWENTY-DONNY

HOTTEST. Haircut. Ever.

Okay, so pretending I was unaware of Ryan was clearly not going to work.

I knew it.

He knew it.

But neither of us seemed inclined to do anything about it.

And wasn't that just the problem?

Confusion and curiosity tangled inside me like over-processed extensions.

I wasn't usually a wishy-washy kind of Witch.

I'd made a decision, hadn't I?

No relationships. No attachments.

That was the deal.

That was what I said.

That was the plan.

But now?

Well, now my mind was screaming one thing, my heart was whispering another, and my body?

Oh, my traitorous body was bellowing louder than them all.

His hands rested gently on my waist.

Not moving.

Not straying.

Not a single thumb brushed lower.

Not a finger dared inch closer to anything inappropriate.

The bearstard! See what I did there? Yeah, I'm forking hilarious.

Somehow, that made it worse. He wasn't copping a feel. He wasn't making a move.

Was something wrong with me? Did he not want me?

No. No, that wasn't it.

I could feel the desire coming off him like heat from a bonfire.

Then why wasn't he acting on it?

Fork. Wait.

Did I want him to?

Surely not.

Right?

I dropped the scissors, suddenly too hot, too aware, too on fire.

My fingers stopped combing through the freshly shorn locks, and when I dared look up—there he was.

Staring.

Big chestnut brown eyes with flecks of gold.

Steady. Unblinking.

Full of something I didn't dare name.

I broke the gaze and lifted the trimmers. I needed something—*anything*—to focus on other than the earthquake rumbling inside me.

That beard had to go.

Ryan remained perfectly still as I worked, eyes dark and glowing with some inner truth.

I used the clippers first, then I picked up my straight razor and sharpened the blade with the rhythm only years of practice could bring, something shifted in him.

His irises flashed golden before turning coal black.

His Bear was close to the surface now, and I couldn't pretend not to feel it.

It thudded like a second heartbeat inside him—and I'd be lying if I said it didn't echo inside me, too.

I dipped the brush and applied my hand-whipped

foam to his skin, stroking carefully. Reverently. As if the very act of shaving him was sacred.

Maybe it was.

His chest rumbled with satisfaction when I wiped the blade across his cheek.

I summoned a damp, heated towel from the other side of the room with a flick of my fingers and pressed it gently to his face.

He moaned.

I clenched.

This was fine.

Totally. Fine.

It was only a haircut. A shave. A simple, totally professional grooming service.

Right?

Except he was sitting, and I was standing—*right between his legs*—and he still towered over me.

I kinda loved that.

He made me feel petite and precious and absolutely seen.

His steady gaze burned through me like Dragon's breath, and I could barely breathe as I cleaned his perfect skin.

My magic tingled in my fingers.

Ryan McLeod was no ordinary man or Shifter.

He was beautiful.

And not just in the *oh hey, he's hot* way. No.

Stupid, dangerous, fairytale beautiful.

The kind that made you believe in impossible things.

"Beautiful," I whispered before I could stop myself.

His lips curled. "You have no idea."

My stomach did a somersault worthy of Olympic gold.

Gold sparks fluttered around us, drawn from me like a bee to pollen.

My magic wanted out. It wanted him. It wanted more.

Nope. Not happening. Not today, Satan.

I inhaled sharply and refocused.

Hair. Hair, Donny. You are here to cut hair.

I wrapped my hands around my favorite shears, letting their warmth center me.

Letting him fade.

I pushed all of it—*desire, confusion, longing*—aside.

I went back over his head with scissors and a comb, adding more to the simple cut I began with.

This was what I was good at.

Styling. Shaping. Seeing the soul beneath the surface and bringing it forward through strands and shears.

I channeled the golden warmth of my magic, letting it settle over me like a cloak.

His energy pulsed against mine—steady, steady, welcoming.

The Bear within him stirred, vast and gentle.

And I realized something that shook me to my core.

He wasn't just tolerating this strange Witch pawing through his mane.

He was inviting me in.

The beast inside him had opened the door.

And I didn't want to close it.

Something inside me bent and swayed like a willow in the wind as I layered the front of his hair, trimming it to just graze his bottom lip.

Shorter on the sides and back.

Sleek. Sexy. Him.

I didn't plan. I never did.

I let my client's energy shape the style. But this?

This was more than that. This was intimacy. This was instinct.

This was mine.

When I pushed his head down to trim the back, I lingered between his thighs, refusing to give up my place.

I felt his hands flex at my waist, but still—*still*—he didn't pull me closer.

Didn't rush.

Didn't demand.

I could've wept for the sheer honor of his restraint.

"Excuse me," I whispered, brushing his shoulder as I stepped away.

His grip tightened, and his eyes bled to black.

"I have to use the razor," I added breathlessly. "I'll be back."

He growled something low and desperate as I spun around, and I couldn't help but grin like a giddy schoolgirl.

I finished the rest with mechanical efficiency and magical speed—shaving, trimming, wiping.

My magic swirled in the air like stardust, completely out of my control but still obeying me in the most delicious way.

When I stepped back and looked at him, my jaw nearly hit the floor.

Holy fork.

He looked like he'd stepped out of my wildest fantasy—a fierce warrior, a devoted protector, a rugged fairytale prince dipped in cinnamon and wrapped in man.

"Well?" he asked, brows raised.

My mouth opened.

Closed.

Then opened again.

"Holy fork," I whispered, dazed.

He laughed. "Did you just say fork?"

"Uh huh."

He tilted his head. "What do utensils have to do with this?"

Even his confusion was sexy.

That was it.

That was my breaking point.

The big, beautiful Bear had waited long enough.

He'd been patient. Kind. Gentle.

And I, well, I was forking done pretending I didn't want him.

My magic was a symphony.

My desire, a scream.

Every inch of my body buzzed with longing.

I flicked my hand, locking the door and flipping the sign to read CLOSED.

Ryan's dark eyes tracked the motion, his nostrils flaring.

"Donny," he growled, voice low and reverent. "Are you sure?"

Was I sure?

No.

Yes.

Absolutely not.

Definitely.

"Shut up, McLeod," I said softly.

Then I kissed him.

CHAPTER TWENTY-ONE- DONNY

"WOW," he whispered, as I lifted my head.

I agreed. Yes. That was so *wow*.

My stomach clenched—*tight, nervous, electric.*

Anticipation wasn't just part of the experience, it was half the magic. And right then, every fiber of my body was screaming that I'd waited long enough.

"Look, Bear," I said, voice low, trembling with something that felt dangerously close to longing. "I'm not sure about anything. But if I don't keep kissing you right now, I'm going to regret it. Whatever else happens, happens. We're adults, right?"

"We are that," Ryan murmured, voice like velvet dipped in sin.

That was good enough for me.

Before I could take another breath, his enormous hands settled on my hips and tugged me forward.

Firm, possessive, but not pushy.

He touched me like he'd been born to hold me.

It should've sent me running.

It didn't.

My eyes were glazed with want and my brain—usually so sharp, so logical—was a melting mess of static and heat.

When had this happened?

When had I started aching for him, not just in my body but somewhere deeper?

Maybe it didn't matter.

His mouth met mine, and the whole world went still.

Just still.

The kind of kiss that turns off time.

The kind of kiss that burns a blueprint into your soul.

Clean rain and cinnamon sugar and something uniquely Ryan—*something warm, male, safe and wild all at once*—wrapped around me like a blanket I didn't know I'd needed.

I moaned as he tilted my head, deepening the kiss, his hand threading into my braid with this quiet sort of reverence that shattered me more than if he'd just grabbed me and claimed me outright.

It was gentle and tender and so heartbreakingly intimate that my chest cracked open.

Oh, Goddess. Could my Bear kiss.

I felt the vibrations in his chest as he growled his pleasure, and it did something to me.

It called something inside me to life.

Something *raw* and *hungry* and *his*.

And still—*still*—his hands didn't stray.

They didn't slide lower.

Didn't grab or grope or grovel.

They held me steady, respectful, strong.

Which somehow made it worse.

Because I wanted more. Needed more. Needed him.

Was something wrong with me? Or was there something so right about this it scared me?

Because I knew what this was. I knew what that voice inside was whispering.

Fated.

I pulled back to catch my breath, to clear my head, to deny the truth I already knew.

But Ryan just sat there, gazing at me with those warm, chestnut eyes ringed in gold, like I was something precious.

Something chosen.

Guilt threatened to overwhelm me, and a flash of regret for all the time I'd wasted trying not to feel this. To block it out. To pretend that what was happening here wasn't real.

"None of that now, Honey," he whispered, moving his mouth, sliding his tongue against mine in a duel as old as time.

Geezus. He was so good at this.

The way his magic pulled at mine? The way my body answered his touch before I'd even told it to move?

These were things I couldn't fake.

His hair curled around my fingers as I ran my hands through his thick locks, and my breath hitched.

I'd left it longer on top. On purpose.

Maybe because I knew I'd want to do exactly this.

I sucked his lip into my mouth, teasing with my teeth.

His answering growl rumbled right through me. I felt it in my bones.

This was crazy. We were practically strangers, but here I was ready to climb him like a mountain —and for some insane reason, I was so there for that.

"We're not strangers, Honey," Ryan rumbled into my mouth. "We're mates."

His voice—low, certain—echoed in my head like a spell.

I wanted to argue.

I wanted to scream that I wasn't ready for this.

That I didn't believe in fairytales.

That I didn't believe in fate.

But those were lies.

Because my magic believed.

And my body sure as fork did.

And that terrifying, treacherous place inside my chest—*the one I'd boarded up and buried years ago*—was listening now.

Even as I denied it with my words, every cell in my body recognized him.

"No," I whispered. "Fuck buddies, maybe. But not mates."

"You're wrong. And I'm gonna prove it to you."

His growl was pure heat, vibrating through every inch of me as he pulled me closer, grinding my body against his thick, hot need.

I gasped, shocked at how ready—*how desperate*—I was.

His restraint should have reassured me.

It didn't.

It drove me wild.

Because I could feel how much he wanted me. I could feel how close he was to snapping.

I rocked my hips again, teasing us both, and my magic flared like sparks on my fingertips. I could taste his hunger. I could feel mine.

The tension snapped.

He stood, lifting me effortlessly, carrying me across the room to press me against the wall. His strength made me feel weightless and wanted and wicked.

We kissed like we were starving.

We kissed like we'd been waiting lifetimes.

Clothes were nothing but an obstacle.

Magic danced around me as I stripped us both with a single flick of power.

"Oh, fork," I gasped as his skin touched mine—*hot and hard and alive.*

"Your magic is so fucking hot," he groaned.

And then he was lowering me onto him.

Yes. YES! But no.

What the fork?

He paused, eyes glowing, voice hoarse.

"Not yet."

I almost cried.

"Why?"

He grinned, infuriating and sexy. "Because I'm a Bear, Honey. And I want to taste you first."

And then he knelt.

The sight of this enormous, powerful man on his knees for me stole the air from my lungs.

His hands wrapped around my thighs, lifting them to his broad shoulders as his mouth moved closer to my center.

My head hit the wall with a thunk.

He stopped, growling as he stood and lifted me, dropping me onto a nearby chair instead.

His concern touched me. Ryan rubbed my head, kissed it, and I nodded, spreading my legs and shoving his shoulders down, waiting for him to take the hint.

He did.

And he fell face first into my pussy, inhaling me like I was his favorite meal, and then, those lips—his crazy bearish lips were tugging at my clit, and I went wild.

"Oh, fuck!"

I opened my eyes, waiting for pink lightning to strike, but the Goddess—*bless her*—gave me a reprieve.

Ryan growled, and my eyes met his as those

prehensile lips curled around my hard little nubbin, and holy fork—*my thighs shook.*

My fingers dug into his hair.

My magic sparked and sizzled around us like a golden storm.

"You're so hot for me, Honey. So goddamn sweet."

"Ryan," I moaned, panting as he ate me like a starved man.

Two thick fingers plunged inside me, but it wasn't enough.

"Please," I grunted. Pulling his hair, needing his thick cock to fill me.

"Patience, Honey," he tutted, nuzzling my pussy with his lips and nose. "I'm gonna fill you alright, but I wanna feel you come on my tongue first."

And when I came, it wasn't just an orgasm.

It was a surrender.

A truth.

A bond I could no longer deny.

He didn't stop.

Not until I was sobbing and shaking and clinging to him like he was the only thing anchoring me to this earth.

Which, in that moment, he was.

Because this wasn't just sex.

It wasn't even just magic.

It was him.

Ryan McLeod.

My Bear.

My fated mate.

And whether I was ready or not, this was only the beginning.

CHAPTER TWENTY-TWO-RYAN

RIGHT AFTER DONNY came on my tongue, I lost all sense of control.

I stood between her parted thighs, pumping my cock with one fist like I was a damn teenager, and when I came—*fuck me*—I came hard.

All over her soft belly and lush thighs.

Watching my release coat her body like a brand sent a primal thrill through me.

Mine.

Goddess help me, she looked perfect like that.

Glowing with orgasm, magic humming off her skin, covered in my scent.

The slick shine of my cum on her curves only made my dick harder.

And she didn't look mad.

She looked hungry.

"Holy fork," she panted, those gorgeous eyes locked on my still-rigid length. "That was so good, so—"

Her voice trailed off like she couldn't even find the words.

Her chest rose and fell with each rapid breath.

Lust. Wonder. Maybe even a little awe.

Made a bear want to pound his chest and roar into the night sky.

Same, Honey. Same.

Because that?

That wasn't just sex.

That wasn't just me showing off my oral skills—though I damn well should've gotten a medal for that performance.

That was everything.

That was the turning point.

The beginning of the bond I'd been aching to forge since the moment I laid eyes on her.

Having sexy fun times with Donny in her after-hours salon? Yeah, it was steamier than anything I'd ever experienced—and I wasn't exactly inexperienced.

But she was different.

She was mine.

Probably because she's my fated mate.

The truth echoed through me, deep and dangerous.

If I wasn't careful, I was going to lose a piece of myself to this woman.

Then again, it was likely already too late.

I lowered my head, pressing my face between her thighs, savoring the taste of her still on my tongue.

Her magic still buzzed against my skin.

Then, I licked her again—slow, possessive, savoring the shiver that ran through her entire body.

"That's a good mate," I growled, standing back up and giving her pretty pussy a tap on my way up.

"I'm not your mate," she shot back instantly, but the words were hollow.

Even she didn't believe them.

"You are," I said, firm but gentle. "But I can wait till you're ready. Bears can be patient."

I let her legs slide closed and helped her lower them slowly to the floor.

Then I yanked her off the chair and into my arms —*sticky mess and all*—and I kissed her deep.

Claimed her mouth like it was the only thing keeping me alive.

And for one perfect second, she kissed me back like she needed me just as badly.

Her arms wrapped tight around me, clutching me like she didn't want to let go.

When our kiss slowed down, I pressed my face to the crook of her neck—right where I intended to bite someday. The spot where my mark would rest.

Her scent was in my lungs. Her thoughts, loud and sweet and sassy, curled around mine.

She was still reeling.

Still trying to figure out what this was, what we were.

But she couldn't lie to herself forever.

Not when I'd made her come twice.

Not when her body had opened to me like a prayer.

And not when her soul was already reaching for mine.

I kissed her temple slowly and reverently and then stepped back.

It was so fucking hard to do that, but I did. Because this was too big for me to rush it. Too important.

She blinked up at me, dazed and deliciously flushed. "What are you doing? Where are you going?"

I bent down, grabbing my pants and shirt. "It's getting late—"

"Late? A second ago you were going at me like you were Pooh, and I was a pot of honey."

"You are the sweetest honey I've ever tasted, Donatella," I said, completely serious.

Her mouth dropped open, and her scent spiked with confusion, want, and frustration.

"Seriously. Where are you going?"

"Home," I said again.

It was the truth. Just not the whole truth.

Her eyes narrowed. "What?"

"The sun's already set, and it's getting late," I said again, softer this time. "But I'd like to walk you home first."

"Listen up, Boo-Boo," she seethed, taking a step forward—completely naked and utterly fearless. "It's not late. It's barely eight o'clock!"

"I have to be at the bakery early," I offered.

She lifted a perfectly arched brow and stalked up to me, her curvy, glorious body on full display.

She jabbed a finger right into my chest.

"Look, Yogi, I can find my own way home. I don't need you to walk me."

I couldn't help it—*I grinned.*

She was adorable when she was pissed.

"You know what, Baloo?" she snapped. "I don't need you to walk me, or to finish *this* either."

She waved her hand and—*bam*—we were both fully clothed again. I growled in irritation.

Like I had any damn right to be mad.

I just tasted heaven, and this woman was somehow driving me insane with lust and pissing me off at the same time.

"I've got plenty of toys at home," she added with a sassy little flip of her hair, "to give me what I need—"

That got a rise out of me.

Literally.

I surged forward and grabbed her, lifting her off the floor and pressing my mouth to hers in a brutal, claiming kiss.

Our tongues tangled.

Her hands dug into my shoulders. I growled, and she bit me—*gently, but it made me see stars.*

I was so damn close to coming again just from her mouth that I almost—*almost*—got embarrassed.

Almost.

I pulled back just far enough to speak, my voice low and guttural.

"No toys unless I'm the one using them on you. No other men. Or women, if that's your thing. Nothing, hear me? Not a single thing," I snarled, the words ripped from deep inside. "Nothing else will ever give you what you need, Donny."

She froze in my arms.

"I'm the only one for you. You can deny it, curse me out, use every name in the bear cartoon universe —but *we* are *destined*."

I kissed her one last time.

Soft, slow, sure.

Then I set her down gently, turned around, and walked right out the door.

My hands were shaking.

I pressed my fingertips to my lips.

"Fucking hell," I muttered.

I was seconds away from losing my hold.

From letting the beast take over.

I hadn't even realized how close I was until it was too late.

The shift came hard and fast.

One moment, I was a man.

The next, my beast broke free.

The great Grizzly Bear roared into the night, scaring the hell out of a poor raccoon digging through the bins behind the bakery.

My paws hit the pavement with a heavy thud-thud-thud, and I ran like hell, trying to outrun the impossible thing that was happening to me.

I turned just in time to see her at the door, eyes glowing, watching me—*really watching me*—

with that same war between curiosity and confusion.

And then, without a word, she disappeared into the salon.

Gone. Just like that.

But I knew this wasn't over.

Not yet. Not ever.

Donny wasn't done with me.

And I sure as fuck wasn't finished with her.

Not even close.

CHAPTER TWENTY-THREE—DONNY

I WAS TOO AMPED up to walk—no way my feet were touching the ground after that Bear blew my freaking mind—then left me there, like yesterday's newspaper.

So, I flew home.

Literally.

Zipped right through the skies of Castor's Corner like a sugar-high Valkyrie on a caffeine bender.

I didn't even bother with a landing spell.

Just dropped out of the air and thudded into my front lawn like a half-buzzed superheroine who'd lost her cape.

Everything in me was vibrating.

My skin, my lips, my—well, let's just say the

entire southern hemisphere was still singing hallelujahs.

I'd just been eaten out by a Bear Shifter with the mouth of a god and the patience of a saint.

And I still didn't know what to do about it.

The only thing I did know?

I was not ready to see the mess waiting for me inside.

But too bad for me, because as soon as I opened the door, I was greeted by the familiar scent of singed leather, mischief, and magical madness.

My house looked like a poltergeist party had collided with a biker bar clearance sale.

Again.

"Still blonde, Witchy?" Gryn snarked from the corner, his voice dripping with smug superiority.

The little turd was perched on my vintage velvet ottoman, tearing metal studs from the authentic 1980s biker boots I just scored at a Chelsea flea market.

We're talking six-hundred-dollar secondhand leather.

Imported. Distressed. Pre-owned by an actual Hell's Angel—probably.

"Yes! I am still blonde!" I snapped, slamming the

door behind me with a flick of my wrist. "How did you do that, anyway?"

My voice came out a little breathless.

Okay, maybe still brain-dead from coming so hard I saw constellations.

So sue me.

Gryn just snarled and gave me his version of a magical shrug, which involved burping up a spark and throwing a stud at the wall like a dart.

"What do you care, Miss Hoity-Toity Know-It-All?" he grumbled, then returned to his DIY destruction project, shredding what was left of the boot with claws and teeth.

My eye twitched.

Those were going to be the centerpiece of my Fall Equinox outfit, but I didn't have it in me to scream.

I just flipped him the bird.

A big ol' glitter-dusted middle finger.

He let out something between a yowl and a guttural curse in a language I still didn't understand —sounded like he was coughing up gravel and regret.

Per usual, I ignored it.

But Goddess, I really needed to start learning whatever forsaken dialect that little Domodork spoke.

Maybe Drusilla offered a familiar language elective at her online Academy?

She knew everything.

I mean, the woman could translate Ghost moaning into operatic arias.

Worth asking.

Mental note made.

But at that moment? I was running on pure magical fumes.

I tossed my keys into the portal-bowl by the door (it burped, rude), kicked off my heels, and sank into my couch with a groan.

Still blonde.

Still grumbling.

Still reeling.

My body was humming from Ryan's touch, but my heart? My head?

They were a tangled mess of what-the-fork-just-happened.

Because somewhere between the teasing and the tongue and the whispered *mate*, I'd felt it.

Felt the bond.

Felt the click.

Felt, er, something.

Something more than sex.

Something bigger than my skepticism and

stronger than the walls I'd built around my heart.

And that? That scared the absolute forking hell out of me.

Gryn cackled in the corner.

So, I flipped him the bird again.

Next, I floated into my bedroom like a Ghost on a sugar crash. The familiar swirl of cool blues and warm yellows hugged me like a weighted blanket for my soul.

This room was my haven.

My retreat.

My carefully curated, color-coordinated fuck off, world space.

Big-ass windows faced the backyard, letting in just the right amount of moonlight to keep the shadows honest. I'd designed this room to be light and airy, a literal breath of fresh air from the rest of my chaotic, magical, Domovyk-destroyed life.

The rest of the house may have been battered by centuries of Andrews family history, but this room was mine.

This entire house was technically mine.

It had been in the family for over two hundred years, passed down from Witch to Witch like a really haunted heirloom—*except ours came with a secret pantry, a Ghost cat in the attic, and a magical plumbing system that flushed backwards during Mercury retrograde.*

Classic Castor's Corner.

My ancestors had come to the New World fleeing persecution and seeking opportunity.

Some came from a long-forgotten village in central Italy—seriously, the actual name's lost to history, which feels like a metaphor for everything else I pretend not to care about.

Like fate.

Or love.

Or gigantic, croissant-baking Bear Shifters with bedroom eyes and a soft spot for mouthy Witches.

Weirdly specific, I know.

But he'd gotten under my skin like splinters from a cursed broom handle.

I sighed and dropped my head in my hands, ignoring the faint char marks Gryn had left on my handcrafted throw rug.

The little turd was probably nesting in the pantry again, chewing on my vintage cake toppers or reorganizing my canned potions alphabetically.

Whatever.

I needed space.

This house had always held both comfort and Ghosts.

My parents hadn't wanted it after my grandparents passed—said it held too many memories.

Maybe they were right, but I couldn't let it go.

Not the wraparound porch with its rocking chairs, not the enormous kitchen where Bella and I brewed love spells disguised as jam.

Not the garden where I poured my energy into the earth and it gave me healing herbs and sweet tomatoes in return.

This place knew me. And I'd built a life here. One where I could thrive without needing anyone.

Or so I'd told myself.

Until him.

Until tonight.

I slammed the bedroom door with a flick of my fingers and locked it tight.

Not that anyone could get in—*there were six protection wards on this room alone*—but I needed the closure. Literal and emotional.

My king-sized bed, a family heirloom carved by my great-grandfather, sat like a throne in the center of the room.

The engraved pine trees and bears had always been my favorite detail.

Go figure.

Guess my subconscious knew something I didn't.

I waved the pillows into a neat pile, shoved back the covers, and climbed in, hoping the thick yellow comforter would soothe the ache Ryan left behind.

And not just the ache in my heart.

I still couldn't believe the man had left. Left. After all that foreplay. After I melted into a puddle on his face.

After I basically threw myself at him like some oversexed groupie at a Shifter bachelor auction.

He walked away.

Who does that?

I was so mad I could spit.

Or cry.

Or combust.

But instead, I reached for my side drawer, ready to prove him wrong.

Ready to show my own damn body that I didn't need a possessive Bear and his magic mouth to feel good.

But when I opened the drawer, my stomach dropped.

Nothing appealed.

Not my trusty lavender wand.

Not my glittery rabbit with three vibration settings.

Not even the obsidian one Evie bought me as a

gag gift but turned out to be very effective.

I stared at my collection of pleasure wands, each more magical than the last, and slammed the drawer shut with a growl.

"That hairy-assed fucker jinxed me!" I hollered.

Zap!

The lightning bolt from the Goddess zapped me square on the ass, leaving a tingling welt and a very bruised ego.

"Ow!" I whined, rubbing my butt as I flopped back on the bed like a tragic heroine in a soap opera. "That wasn't even that bad a curse word!"

And there I was.

Still blonde.

Still horny.

Still furious.

I tugged the comforter up and rolled onto my side, trying to summon sleep. But the second I closed my eyes, I saw him.

Ryan.

His eyes. His hands.

The way he looked at me.

The way he kissed like he was memorizing my mouth with his soul.

The way he didn't stay.

I knew he wanted me to say it.

To claim him back.

To admit we were mates.

But I wasn't ready.

I didn't know if I'd ever be ready.

Because the moment I said those words, I wouldn't be Donny Andrews, Trifecta Witch, owner of Hair Now, Gone Tomorrow, reigning queen of independence and glitter eyeliner.

I'd be *his.*

And I didn't know if I could survive losing myself.

Even if he made me feel more alive than anyone ever had.

I inhaled deeply. Exhaled slowly.

The sheets smelled like cedar and rosemary. Comforting.

I wanted them to smell like him, though.

I buried my face in the pillow and muttered, "Puhleeeze," like the world was trying to sell me the fantasy of true love and I was the last Witch on Earth not buying it.

But deep down?

Yeah.

Part of me was already sold.

CHAPTER TWENTY-FOUR-DONNY

SEE, I knew Witches and Shifters could mate.

That wasn't some big mystical revelation or forbidden love plot twist.

Biologically, magically, and cosmically—it was all on the up and up.

The great La Befana herself, Magdelena the Magnificent, had a Shifter mate and two gorgeous sets of twins with glowing eyes and prophecy written into their DNA.

Hell, those kids were destined to one day lead the magical world into a new era of peace and power.

Or at least that's what the CovenNet forums said.

And everyone knows if it's on CovenNet, it's probably true.

But here in Castor's Corner?

I'd seen it firsthand.

Evie and Jaxson were the blueprint.

My best friend—*the town's big boss mayor*—shacked up with our sexy new Wolf Sheriff, and from all accounts, they were happy.

Fated. Cozy even.

So yes. It could happen.

Just not to me.

Because I wasn't mate material.

Not even close.

I didn't have a maternal bone in my body—unless you counted my firm belief that every being, magical or mortal, should have access to good leave-in conditioner.

Shifter men? They were basically giant, hairy toddlers with six-packs.

Did I look like the type of woman who wanted to babysit a brooding Bear just to keep him from stomping off into the woods every time he got cranky?

I don't even babysit my familiar properly.

Gryn runs feral 90% of the time and chews on my favorite shoes like a furry Gremlin with a grudge.

Besides, looking at the disaster that was my family tree? Fidelity was more of a suggestion than a practice.

The Andrews and the Castors—we weren't exactly known for sticking it out.

Hell, half of us couldn't even pick a hair color and commit.

I knew myself. I knew that I'd never cheat, not on purpose, not in a million lifetimes.

But that didn't stop the gnawing voice in my head.

The one that whispered things like what if it's in your blood?

What if there's some wild, restless, cursed seed buried deep in my DNA that would one day take root and ruin everything?

The thought made my stomach cramp and my heart twist.

I hated it.

Hated me for even thinking it.

When I was a kid, Granny Andrews used to look at me like I was some kind of delicate mistake.

Always criticizing the way I dressed, the way I talked, the friends I made, the boys I liked.

She'd whisper her disapproval like it was a hex, but only when my parents weren't around. Subtle, but poison all the same.

And when I turned twenty and came home from college to announce—*with sparkly eye shadow and righteous conviction*—that I was dropping out to go to beauty school?

Whew. That was the cherry on her judgment sundae.

"A real Witch uses her power to protect the world, not dye roots and curl bangs," she'd sneered.

Well, fork her.

Fork her twice for making me feel like crap.

It had taken me years—*literal years and one heart-shaped handheld mirror*—to finally believe I was good at what I did.

That what I did mattered.

That making someone feel beautiful could be a kind of healing.

That being a stylist, a potion crafter, a business owner, and a damn good friend was enough.

But being someone's mate? Could I do that?

I wasn't so sure.

Especially not Ryan's.

That Bear of a man was too solid.

Too good. Too real.

The kind of person who deserved a warm-hearted, nurturing mate who made casseroles and sewed buttons and never once considered running off to Bermuda to open a potion bar on a whim.

He deserved better than a moody, magically

unstable stylist with control issues and commitment phobia.

I worried my bottom lip until it was sore, and glared at the drawer full of abandoned toys like they were traitors to the cause.

"I'm a forking mess," I muttered.

Maybe being alone was just safer.

Plenty of Witches went that route.

The Chickie twins had never mated.

They had each other, a pair of matching orthopedic shoes, and a legacy of enchanted lawn ornaments that could out-sing Mariah Carey.

And then I made the mistake of picturing myself thirty years from now.

In a shapeless violet housecoat, mismatched knee-highs, half a dozen rollers clamped in my still-blonde hair—*because of course the hair would still be blonde.*

Maybe Gryn would be perched on my shoulder gnawing on my retirement paperwork, and no Ryan in sight.

I screamed.

Like, internally screamed, but loud enough for my soul to hear.

"That's it," I growled, marching toward the master

bathroom with dramatic flair. "I'm fixing this hair now."

Enough was enough.

If I couldn't fix my future, I could at least fix my damn roots.

So what if it was risky?

What was the worst that could happen?

CHAPTER TWENTY-FIVE-RYAN

I SLAMMED the door to the rental so hard the frame rattled.

Didn't care.

Should have been curled around my mate right now, full belly, full heart, peace in my bones.

Instead?

I was cold. Horny. Miserable. And alone.

Not that Conrad noticed.

"Dude," he called from the couch, not even looking up from the massive python coil he had twisted himself into. "You smell like sex and forest. What gives?"

"Fuck. Off." I stomped past him, stripping my shirt off as I headed for the shower.

I barely noticed the chill as the pipes screamed and dumped liquid ice over my overheated skin.

The hot water heater was still busted—Bella had said something about magical backflow or a tiny volcano in the tank. I couldn't remember.

Didn't matter.

I stood under the freezing spray, letting it punish me while I scrubbed every inch of skin with the tiny white bar of Ivory soap.

No scent. No trace. Nothing to remind me of her.

Didn't help.

I was clean.

But I wasn't okay.

When the soap bar slipped from my fingers, whittled down to nothing, I let it go.

Let it circle the drain and disappear, like the last hour of my life hadn't changed everything.

Because it had.

I'd tasted her.

Had her trembling and gasping on my tongue.

And then I'd left.

On purpose.

Which was probably the dumbest, most painful thing I've ever done.

But I had to.

Because if I stayed, I would've claimed her right

there in that damn salon chair, in the heat of her magic and mine.

I'd have knotted inside her and bitten her and never let go.

And she wasn't ready.

Hell, she couldn't even say the word *mate*.

I yanked on a clean T-shirt and sweats, combed my fingers through my damp hair, and trudged back into the living room where Conrad was still mid yoga pose—*coiled into what looked like a sentient pretzel.*

Snake Shifters, man. No shame.

"What's up?" he asked, not even glancing away from the TV, which was playing some black-and-white movie about two lovers who couldn't make it work.

Fitting.

I dropped onto the armchair across from him with a heavy grunt.

"I need to woo this woman, Con. I just don't have a clue how."

That got his attention. He straightened slightly, human torso emerging from his twisty lower half.

"I thought you were in after tonight? You reek of her magic and croissant crumbs."

"She won't admit we're mates," I said, rubbing the

heel of my hand against my sternum like I could press the ache away. "Says we're fuck buddies, at best."

"Ouch." Conrad winced. "She said that out loud?"

I nodded once.

He gave a low whistle and untangled himself with the grace of someone boneless. "Damn. So, what now?"

"I don't know. That's the problem. I've never *wooed* anyone before. Not like this." I leaned forward, elbows on knees.

"She's got walls. Not little ones either. Like castle battlements. With magical firepower and maybe a catapult."

"You like her that much?"

"She's it," I said simply. "There's no one else. There never will be."

Conrad exhaled slowly.

"Then you're gonna have to be patient, my dude. Witchy women don't like to be cornered. But if you find out how to make one see reason? Let me know. My future mate still doesn't acknowledge me unless it's to zap me when I open my big mouth."

I cracked a half-smile. "Donny doesn't zap me."

"Yet."

"True."

Silence stretched between us. I could still smell her on my skin, even after the cold-water punishment.

Her magic had wrapped around mine and sunk in deep.

There was no shaking it.

No going back.

I needed a plan.

Not just a strategy to win her over, but one that told her I saw her.

All of her.

Not just the smart-ass Witch with the attitude and killer curves—*but the scared, proud, loyal woman underneath.*

"Flowers?" I said aloud, brow furrowing.

Conrad snorted. "She'll think you're apologizing for cheating on her with her sister or something."

"True."

"Cookies?" he offered.

"Her bestie owns a bakery. She can get them anytime."

"Fuck."

More silence.

Then, like lightning hitting a pine tree, I had it.

"I'm going to make her something special," I said, sitting up straighter.

"Oh?"

"A gift. Something real. No spells, no charm. Just me. My hands. My time."

Conrad gave a low whistle again. "You're gonna woodwork her into loving you?"

"If I have to. But not wood. I'm thinking flour and butter," I grunt.

Because that's what Bears do.

We build.

We fix.

We protect.

And even if she didn't believe in fate yet, that was okay.

Because I did.

And Donatella Andrews was mine.

CHAPTER TWENTY-SIX-DONNY

WHAT COULD GO WRONG?

Famous. Forking. Last. Words.

I stood in front of the salon's vintage mirror, flicking my fingers through my newly-restored golden honey waves.

Thank the Goddess the clown show had left the building.

My hair was finally behaving again—*no more rainbow coils, no more Bozo curls, and no more magical meltdowns in the middle of deep-conditioning treatments.*

The last two days had been hell.

Rainbow perm hell.

I hadn't just singed my pride, I'd nuked it with that impulsive attempt to undo Gryn's blonde curse.

And yes, I had resembled a circus reject for 48 straight hours.

Even Celeste had flinched the first time she saw me.

The little Domovyk had howled with laughter, rolling around on my designer rug like he was possessed.

"You like blonde better, Witchy?" he'd sneered this morning, smug and smugger in his ripped leather vest.

"Yes, I like blonde better, you groin-Goblin," I snapped back, dragging my coffee to my lips like it owed me rent.

He just went back to yanking the metal studs out of a $800 vintage Armani jacket.

I flipped him off and cursed him with the itchiest ear hair known to familiar-kind.

He deserved it.

But no more self-doubt.

No more groveling to fate or flinching at the sight of my own reflection.

Today was a new day, and I was a Witch with work to do and bills to pay.

"Hair Now, Gone Tomorrow, this is Celeste speaking!" chirped my blue-haired assistant from the front desk, her voice perkier than a caffeinated bunny rabbit.

I rolled my eyes and smiled despite myself. I might've been cranky, frustrated, and dangerously horny thanks to one stubborn-ass Bear Shifter who ruined me for adult toys, but I loved this place.

My shop. My sanctuary.

And I wasn't going to let some moody man-Bear or evil Imp-familiar unravel me.

Not today.

I'd earned this life. I'd built this business.

I was Donatella Andrews, Witch of the Trifecta, protector of Castor's Corner, and badass stylist to the supernatural stars.

I'd tamed Troll beards, Shifter manes, and the occasional possessed extension. I could handle this.

Even if *this* included complete cherry turnover withdrawal and a libido stuck on fuck or combust.

Because, yeah—I'd been skipping the bakery.

But *someone—not naming that giant Bear-sized rock in my shoe right now*—had sent me a dozen cherry turnovers with vanilla glaze and a sticky note that read:

When you're ready to accept we're

mates, call me. But not until then, Honey.
I can wait for you.
-Ryan

Smug. Assface.

I didn't burn the box, but I thought about it. Instead, I ate all twelve pastries in one sitting, washed them down with half a bottle of Chianti, and rage-watched season one of Game of Thrones. Twice.

I still wasn't over the *Red Wedding*.

But I was still not anyone's forking mate.

Gold sparks flared at my fingertips again, heat rising behind my sternum.

Inhale. Exhale.

I wasn't mad because of what Ryan said. I was mad because a part of me believed him.

My magic did too, and it hated being denied.

But I wasn't ready.

Not to be claimed, not to be tied to anyone, and sure as fork not to lose myself again in someone else's shadow.

So when Celeste bounced over and announced, "The Chicky twins are here!" with a too-bright smile, I bit back a groan.

"Send them in," I said through gritted teeth.

"Look what the—" Candice began.

"—cat dragged in," Denice finished with a synchronized sigh.

"Nice to see you finally taking responsibility," Candice continued.

"We thought stylists had to work to make money," Denice added, pursing her wrinkled lips.

I smiled.

Sharp. Cold.

The kind of smile that said I could turn them into toads if I wanted.

"Ladies," I greeted with a nod. "Here for your free weekly dose of passive aggression?"

They gasped in unison. It was glorious.

Celeste choked behind the counter, pretending to cough.

"We're only here—" Candice began.

"—because you messed up our hair—" Denice added.

"As usual," Candice finished.

That was it. I'd had it.

"Really? Messed up, huh? Well, I see two perfectly styled, root-touched-up heads with not a gray in sight," I continued. "Now, unless you're here to book a real appointment—*and pay for it*—Celeste will schedule you for your monthly pedicure. Otherwise, I have paying clients coming in."

"Well—"

"I never!" they huffed, clutching their matching mustard yellow handbags like they were about to be mugged.

"We'll take our business elsewhere—"

"Until you apologize!"

Then, they walked out, taking eerily matching steps as they shoved through the door.

"Oh, sweet Hecate," Celeste whispered. "That was amazing. You are a Goddess."

"Nope," I said with a grin. "Just a Witch who's officially done taking anyone's shit. And I've let those two walk all over me for years!"

She laughed and clapped, bouncing in her combat boots. "Pizza for lunch?"

"Only if it's greasy, cheesy, and bad for my chakras."

"Thought you'd never ask."

As Celeste ordered, I leaned back in my chair, finally letting my shoulders drop.

The lightning in my chest had faded, and for the first time in days, I felt like myself again.

Maybe I didn't have all the answers.

Maybe I wasn't ready to be someone's mate.

But I was ready to consider the possibility.

And I was so forking done letting fear make my choices for me.

"Celebratory pizza has been ordered!" Celeste cheered.

She was really something else.

And by *something else*, I meant she'd vacillated between cheerleading me with cult-level enthusiasm and avoiding me like I was the second coming of the rainbow hair disaster.

I couldn't exactly blame her.

I'd been cranky, twitchy, and not-so-quietly vibrating with barely contained sexual tension all day. Even *I* was annoying myself.

Still, she stuck it out.

I had three remaining clients today, two emergency walk-ins (one of them a Troll with sideburns like steel wool), and somehow, we made it through.

I was grateful for the chaos. Truly.

Work was the only thing keeping me from spontaneously combusting into a glittery cloud of magical angst and sexually frustrated pheromones.

Unfortunately, even trimming Hedgehog Shifter hair and mixing a fresh batch of lilac-sage scalp soother couldn't fully distract me from *him*.

The sexy, brooding Bear Shifter with a tongue

like sin and a voice that sounded like it had been soaked in bourbon and rolled in flannel.

I caught myself zoning out more than once during appointments, and let me tell you, imagining Grizzlies going down on Witches while holding scissors near someone's ears? *Not advisable.*

At last, it was the end of the day. I swept up the last of the enchanted curls and dead ends and hit the *start* button on the magical crematorium under the sink, watching the hair clippings vanish in a puff of lavender smoke.

Satisfying.

Celeste gave me a tight-lipped smile, tucked her bag under her arm, and bolted before I could say anything about a staff drink or snack.

I should've felt bad.

Instead, I muttered, "Good call," to no one in particular, locked up, and headed out.

I needed air. A walk. Anything to stop thinking about his mouth.

The breeze hit me the second I stepped outside, crisp and cool, smelling like leaves and apples and fireplace smoke. *October in Castor's Corner.* It was pure magic.

Storefronts were done up for spooky season—hay bales, gourds, grinning pumpkins, glam-witch mannequins in corseted dresses, and enough fairy lights to make Times Square look dim.

The town practically hummed with spellwork and nostalgia, a mix of normal and not-so-normal all wrapped in charm.

Everyone was buzzing about the Halloween Bash, and sure, the seasonal display game was strong —but I wasn't really feeling it this year.

Evie wanted a "Hollywood Bombshells" theme, and while I normally lived for vintage glam, I didn't want to spend the entire night being compared to every blonde Witch from history.

Especially not Marilyn.

Don't get me wrong—I was adjusting.

The blonde thing?

I was starting to see the appeal.

It looked soft in the lamplight, a mix of ash and gold, the kind of color people paid thousands for. It even brought out the odd tones in my eyes—a brownish hazel that skewed mossy green in the morning and wolfish gold at dusk.

I used to think they were my best feature.

Well. Before *he* showed up and made me question every inch of my body and soul.

I crossed my arms and kept walking.

My heels—*Prada, thank you very much*—clicked

against the sidewalk as I strolled past the bakery (yes, *that* bakery), refusing to glance at it, even though I knew full well the smell of cinnamon and warm cherry glaze would wreck me.

My Armani jeans clung like a second skin, enchanted to elongate my legs and lift my ass just so.

Paired with the vintage off-shoulder lace blouse I found in Paris during my failed escape-from-Castor's-Corner years ago, and yeah, I looked *good*.

But what did it matter?

It didn't matter how I looked or what kind of potion I brewed or how many clients I booked. I was still just me.

Donatella Andrews. Stylist. Witch. Daughter of disappointingly normal parents. Granddaughter of one of the grumpiest, most judgmental Witches ever to haunt a rocking chair.

Granny always said I was too soft. Too dreamy. Too full of nonsense.

When I quit college to enroll in beauty school, she declared I was throwing my life away.

My parents, bless them, came around eventually.

But Granny? She always thought I'd end up barefoot and crying, alone in a house full of cats and unpaid bills.

I clutched my arms tighter around myself and slowed as I reached the edge of the park.

Funny thing was, I *did* come back. And not barefoot. Not broken.

I bought the shop from those nasty old biddies, the Chickee twins.

I built a life.

I healed people in ways they didn't even realize needed healing.

Hair magic wasn't just glamour—it was restoration.

It was self-worth. I helped people see the best in themselves.

So why couldn't I see it in me?

Maybe the town didn't hate me.

Maybe I just hadn't stopped believing my Granny's voice long enough to listen to my own.

I paused, sucking in a deep breath of fall air. The trees above rustled like they were whispering secrets I hadn't heard since I was a kid.

My skin buzzed—not with static, but with something else.

Something low and warm and humming.

Power.

I *was* part of this town. I belonged here.

No man, no prophecy, no glowing mating mark was going to make me forget that again.

Not even the Bear whose kisses made me forget my own name.

But the thing was, he wasn't asking me to give up anything, was he?

Shit. So what if, I was the one who messed up by not giving him a shot?

These were thoughts that needed time and a long stroll to figure out.

So, off I went.

CHAPTER TWENTY-SEVEN- DONNY

THE CEMETERY LOOMED AHEAD, a sprawling patch of lovingly curated earth and stone.

Most people might've found it creepy, but not me.

Castor's Corner wasn't the kind of place where the dead stayed quiet.

And honestly, that was kind of comforting.

A little spooky, yeah, but also proof that this weird, magical town of ours cared.

We honored our dead. Hell, we practically invited them to Sunday dinner.

Graves were well-tended, mausoleums polished, offerings refreshed. Because in Castor's Corner, you never knew who was watching from the *Other Side*— or taking notes.

The Next Amazing Journey was a real thing, and if you thought your mama wouldn't haunt you for letting her roses die, you didn't know Witches.

I wasn't here for any ancestor worship, though. I just needed to walk.

Think. Breathe.

My birthday was tomorrow, and the thought made my stomach twist.

Normally, I'd be planning a spa night with Bella and Evie, maybe matching glam spells and a few bottles of wine, but this year? I didn't want any of it.

Another year gone, and what had I accomplished?

I was still alone.

Still slinging hair potions and dodging emotionally constipated familiars.

Still unsure if I was even worthy of being one-third of the magical Trifecta that protected this town.

I mean, what did I bring to the table?

A mean ombré? A killer pedicure with a long-lasting spell?

Hair might be sacred to Witches, but when it came to stopping ancient curses and magical upheaval? I wasn't exactly a heavy hitter.

And to top it all off, turns out I wasn't even a real Andrews.

Nope. I was a Castor by blood.

Daddy dearest didn't even know, and now I had to decide whether to tell him or pretend this existential identity crisis didn't exist.

Forking crapozoids.

As if summoned by my internal pity party, the Castorini mausoleum appeared around the bend—hulking, elegant, and ominous as ever.

I paused, staring at the names etched into the smooth stone, each one a chapter in the town's legacy.

I circled the structure slowly, fingers trailing over cool marble and ornate carvings.

One plaque was smeared with a splash of mud, right over the name Alfonso Castor.

Figures.

Grandpa Al, even in death, couldn't stay tidy. I rolled my eyes and wiped the mess off with my sleeve.

And that's when the weirdness began.

A low groan echoed from the stone.

I froze.

Just for a second.

Just long enough for every hair on my body to stand at attention.

"Oh no," I whispered. "No, no, no. Don't you dare pull some Scooby-Doo shizzle on me right now."

Thick black smoke started seeping from the name I'd just cleaned, coiling through the air like something straight out of a goth's fever dream.

My heartbeat went full techno-rave. The plumes grew heavier, pulsing with shadows.

I took a step back, then another, because I was brave but not stupid.

"You have got to be forking kidding me."

And then—*because apparently the universe hated me today*—a semi-translucent figure materialized from the smoke.

Grandpa Al. In all his junkless glory.

Looking like death warmed over and then microwaved for good measure.

"Donatella? Sei tu? Is that you, little one?"

His voice was raspy, his form flickering like a busted neon sign.

And okay, yeah, it was definitely him. Right down to the Ghostly hole right where his Ghostly junk should've been.

I winced.

Guess curses didn't stop just because you died.

I cleared my throat and tried not to focus on his missing manhood.

"Uh, yeah. It's me. What the fork is going on? I thought you crossed over?"

He gave a sorrowful little shrug, the kind that said *well, about that.*

"I almost did," he said. "Ivan was helping me. He was channeling the magic, guiding me toward the light. But then? Poof. Gone."

"Poof?" I echoed, blinking.

"Poof," he repeated, voice going all high and squeaky like a helium balloon at a haunted birthday party.

Before I could snark back, the ground trembled beneath me—an actual freaking tremor.

I grabbed a nearby tree for balance.

"Careful, ragazza!"

The shaking passed, but the dread in my chest didn't.

This wasn't just Ghostly weirdness.

This was Big Magic stuff.

Bad juju. Like very bad.

"I've been stuck in the in-between ever since," Grandpa Al said. "I'm tired, Donatella. So tired. I can't reach anyone. Only you."

"Why me?" I asked, completely serious for once. "Why not Evie? Or Bella? I'm just the third wheel on the enchanted tricycle."

"No. You're the key," he said, his voice fading. "You're the one tied to me. You're the one who can set this right."

"Set what right?" I demanded, stepping forward. "You messed around with your mistress, got cursed, and died. And now I have to clean up the cosmic aftermath?"

He blinked at me with watery Ghost eyes. "Please, my bellissima granddaughter. I want to get to the Next Amazing Journey. I don't want to vanish into nothing."

And then he did. Poof—he vanished.

I spun in a circle.

"No, no, no! Don't you Ghost me, old man!"

CRACK!

Thunder overhead.

"Fucking hell!"

I slapped a hand over my mouth too late and ducked behind a tree just as a pink lightning bolt zapped the air where I'd been standing.

"Goddess has no chill," I muttered.

When the sky stopped trying to smite me, I scrambled out of the cemetery, heart pounding, heels clicking, and Ghost-haunted words echoing in my ears.

I was the key?

That was a load of sparkly bullshi—*stuff.*

I wasn't a hero. I was a stylist with a bad temper and a drawer full of battery-operated disappointment.

But deep down—*where the truth likes to whisper*—I knew I couldn't ignore this.

Something was coming. Something big.

And apparently, the only thing standing between my Ghostly grandfather and oblivion was me.

Goddess, help us all.

I closed my eyes and sucked in a breath, trying to gain my bearings.

When, of course, something scared the begeezus out of me.

"Are you alright?"

That voice.

That deep, sexy, gravel-dipped-in-honey voice.

My entire body went stiff. And not the fun kind of stiff, either.

The still-blonde hairs on the back of my neck stood straight up as I whipped around like I was in a horror movie.

Except instead of a chainsaw-wielding lunatic, I was greeted by a very different kind of monster.

A big, sexy, Bear Shifter shaped one.

"What the fork?!"

Ryan McLeod stood just beyond the cemetery gates like something out of a supernaturally sexy lumberjack fashion spread—seven feet of solid Shifter, his green flannel rolled up over those thick forearms I may or may not have dreamed about licking.

The second I turned, he pushed off the wrought iron with a soft smile and wide, hopeful eyes that almost made me forget the Ghost trauma I'd just endured.

Almost.

Then he opened his arms.

That was all it took.

I launched myself at him like a magical missile.

No hesitation, no logic, just pure, unfiltered Donny energy.

And the big guy caught me like I weighed nothing more than a particularly enthusiastic cat.

He spun me once, and I let myself laugh—a real, from-the-gut, spark-shooting laugh I hadn't heard from myself in weeks.

Ryan nuzzled my neck, his nose brushing that ticklish spot beneath my ear, and I almost forgot we were standing next to my dead grandfather's mausoleum.

"I got you, Honey. Easy," he murmured, lips ghosting kisses across my cheek.

My heart squeezed. I could feel happiness flowing into me through our connection.

Not just his—*mine too.*

It was like plugging into a live wire of joy. Damn it.

"I have to call the girls," I said quickly as my feet touched the ground again. "We've got trouble. The Ghost kind."

"Okay, but I'm bringing you to see them," Ryan said without missing a beat. "They're at the firehouse. I was supposed to come get you—"

"Why? What are you hiding?" I cut him off, arms crossing.

Oops, forgot how to behave there for a second. My inner Jersey girl was showing.

"Well, uh, they're planning, um, well, happy birthday, Honey," Ryan said and looked away from my narrowed gaze, scratching the back of his neck in that sexy way all hot boys seem to know.

"A surprise party? Are you forking kidding me? I told them not to!"

"If you don't want to go," Ryan said, all calm and easy, "I'll take you somewhere else. We don't have to stay. Just let me drive you, okay?"

He pointed to a royal blue pickup parked along the cemetery gates.

It gleamed like maybe he'd polished it just for me. *Sweet.*

I rolled my eyes, but the gesture warmed me.

"No, it's fine. We'll go. But we're doing it my way."

Before he could protest, I grabbed his hand and flew us straight to the Castor's Corner Firehouse, magic whipping around us like we were in some kind of supernatural romcom with a high production budget.

We landed with a soft whoosh outside the big brick building, my heels touching down just as the party started yelling inside.

"OMG! She's here! Everyone hide! Dim the lights!" Bella's voice rang out like a panicked squirrel.

Sparkles—*pink and aqua, of course*—blasted across the ceiling like celebratory fireworks on a sugar high.

I stepped through the door, Ryan at my side, and I took in the scene.

Banners, floating cupcakes, shimmering disco balls, and a life-size cutout of me in full stylist regalia holding a curling wand like a weapon.

"For the love of glam," I muttered. "I know about the dang party, Bella," I said loudly over the music.

"Surprise!" Celeste yelled over the mic, and everyone kind of froze with wary smiles on their faces.

"How'd you know?" Bella asked, blue eyes tearing up.

"OMG, Bella, don't cry! You guys throw me one every year even though I beg you not to."

Half the town was there.

Celeste was behind the DJ booth with some guy in a sushi hat—like an actual futomaki handroll on his head.

I couldn't tell if he was supposed to be Wrap or Roll, but he looked thrilled.

Realizing I'd just walked in like a literal thundercloud of magical trauma and bad attitude, I drew a deep breath and softened my voice.

"Thank you, everyone. Sorry for being a-a big ol' party pooper. I really do appreciate it."

Celeste nodded and dropped the beat.

Dr. Dre and Snoop filled the firehouse like it was '94 all over again, and Witches, Warlocks, and Shifters alike started getting their groove on.

I made a beeline for Evie and Bella.

They looked like two guilty puppies caught chewing on spell books.

"Donny," Evie said, wringing her hands. "We're sorry. We just wanted to make you feel special."

Bella's chin wobbled, and I melted. Damn her sweet marshmallow heart.

"No way," I said, grabbing their hands. "I love you both. And even though I didn't want to celebrate my birthday, I'm glad you ignored me. Kind of."

"We're family," Evie said, her voice fierce and her grip tighter. "Always have been."

"She's right," Bella added. "And Donny, not all change is bad. It's been a weird year for all of us, but I think it's time we reinforce our Trifecta bond. Not just for the town, but for us."

I felt it then—my magic stirring.

That low hum I hadn't realized I'd been missing until it came roaring back like a much-needed coffee IV.

Evie grabbed my hand. Bella grabbed the other. We closed the circle.

Power surged.

Comfort. Connection. Love.

We were stronger together. That was the truth. Always had been.

"You know what this means," Evie said, eyes sparkling with danger and disco.

"NO. NO WAY, EVIE CASTOR!" I yelled.

But it was too late.

With a wave of her hand, the music switched.

"It's CONGA TIME!"

Oh, sweet Sparkles. She did it.

Suddenly, the party morphed into a Miami nightmare—Shifters trying to dance in sync, Witches casting sparkles into the air, and Warlocks dodging rogue heels.

I just hoped no one got concussed this year from errant boob-swinging.

"I'm wearing a bra, Donny!" Bella hissed, reading my mind like the Witchy soul sister she was.

"Then Goddess help us all," I muttered, and joined the damn conga line.

Because that's what you do when you've got your girls, your magic, and one absurdly hot Bear waiting just off to the side with a cupcake in one hand and a look in his eyes that promised I was the only thing he'd be unwrapping tonight.

Oh well. Fork it.

If you can't beat 'em, try hitting them with a love spell or a hex! Wasn't that the saying?

Anyway, maybe this birthday wasn't such a bust after all.

CHAPTER TWENTY-EIGHT—RYAN

EVIE'S VOICE boomed through the firehouse like a damn freight train in heels.

She'd clearly used some kind of megaphone spell, and it worked like a charm.

The whole party—*every cackling Witch, every beer-chugging Shifter, every pointy-hatted Warlock and furry-tailed Fae*—paused mid-bite or mid-boogie to turn toward the makeshift stage set up near Engine Two.

I couldn't be mad though.

All of this was for *her*.

My sweet Donny.

And yeah, maybe her actual birthday wasn't for another couple of hours, but you'd never guess it by the way Castor's Corner showed up.

The firehouse was packed to the rafters.

Streamers spelled out her name in floating cursive.

There was glitter in the air and confetti on the floor and a suspiciously lifelike cardboard cutout of Donny wielding a blow dryer like a sword near the buffet table.

She looked mortified.

But I thought she looked like magic.

I took a slow breath, in and out.

Not because I was incensed—but because my chest felt so full, it might just crack open.

This town had a way of wrapping you up and holding you close, and watching them celebrate my Witch—*because yeah, she was mine, even if she hadn't admitted it yet*—made my damn throat tight.

Like I'd swallowed an entire cinnamon stick. *Sideways.*

The music kicked back up, and just like that, the conga line exploded.

"Everybody do the conga!" blared through the speakers, and Witches, Warlocks, Shifters, and even two Domovyks with glow sticks got in formation.

I lost track of how many times we circled the firehouse. The place had like six stories—*don't ask me why*—and I swear we hit every single level. My legs didn't care.

My Bear was too busy watching the way Donny's hips moved to remember we were supposed to be acting cool.

Eventually, I peeled off from the group and found a quiet spot against the cool cement wall next to one of the big red fire trucks.

The engine gleamed, polished to perfection.

It was familiar. Solid.

Kind of like how I wanted to be for her.

I spotted her a second later.

She looked dazzling and out of place all at once, like a celestial being stuck on Earth with nothing but sass and heels to protect her.

Blonde hair glowing in the string lights.

Mouth twitching like she wasn't sure if she wanted to smile or hex someone.

I grabbed two cold beers from a passing cooler cart—*yes, that was a thing here*—and made my way to her like gravity demanded it.

"Thirsty?" I asked, stepping up behind her just as she paused near the firetruck.

She gasped and clutched her chest like I'd startled her. I hadn't meant to, but I wasn't sorry either.

Not when her eyes landed on mine like I was the anchor she didn't realize she needed.

She took the beer with a mumbled "thank you," and our fingers brushed.

Just that tiny touch sent a pulse of heat racing up my arm.

She blinked fast, then looked away, like she wasn't sure what to do with what just passed between us.

But I knew.

I'd known since the first time she looked at me with those hazel eyes that flickered like mood rings and called me a *Grizzly-sized pain in the ass.*

I was hers. Fully. Completely.

And I was ready to wait for her to figure that out.

"What's up, Honey?" I asked gently. "You've been trying to find the right words all night."

She stiffened.

She hadn't told anyone yet.

I could see it in the way her shoulders tensed, like she was carrying too much and pretending it wasn't crushing her.

But I'd seen the signs.

Her pacing. Her distracted smile.

The way her magic sparked in bursts when she thought no one was looking.

"You don't have to say it all now," I added, softer.

"But whatever it is, I'll help you, Donatella. Any way I can."

That made her look at me. Really look.

The air between us shifted.

Something ancient. Something holy.

She opened her mouth, closed it, then nodded.

A deep breath lifted her chest, and I could almost hear the click of something inside her falling into place.

"Right," she said finally, her voice low but clear. "Maybe it's time I started trusting myself. And the people who've shown up for me."

Her gaze lingered on me for a second longer than I thought I could bear without kissing her, then drifted to where Evie and Bella were dancing near the DJ booth.

"They're my ride-or-dies," she said. "Always have been. But you and the guys, you didn't mean to come here. And you didn't have to stay."

I smiled. "Yeah, we did."

She snorted.

"Stubborn Bear."

"Maybe. Or maybe fate's got better aim than you think."

That got me a laugh.

A real one.

And I'd take it.

Because I knew—*whatever storm was coming, whatever darkness she was carrying*—it didn't scare me. Not one bit.

I was here for it.

For her.

Even if she never said the words, I'd be the anchor. The fireproof wall. The growly Shifter with snacks and strength and shoulders wide enough to carry whatever the hell she needed.

Because Donatella Andrews didn't just belong to Castor's Corner.

She belonged to me.

And it was time she realized that.

CHAPTER TWENTY-NINE-
DONNY

I LOOKED UP AT RYAN, his golden-brown eyes steady on mine, calm like the earth after a storm. I didn't say a word, but something passed between us —hot, sure, and ancient.

A promise.

A tether.

And the second he dipped his chin in that almost imperceptible nod, my insides turned molten.

Oh yeah.

This wasn't just lust.

It wasn't even just magic.

He was big. He was steady. He was special.

And if I played my cards right—*and stopped letting fear dictate my every damn move*—he was going to be mine.

But first, I had work to do.

Unfinished business.

Someone I had to help.

Someone I maybe owed.

I turned toward the girls where they stood a few yards away, laughing and chatting with our Shifter shadows, and my voice came out sharper than I intended.

"When I went to the cemetery today, I saw Grandpa Al."

Everything stopped.

"Grandpa Al?" Bella echoed. "He's back? How is that even possible?"

"Well, he never left, actually." I folded my arms, feeling the weight of the truth settle in again.

"He's stuck here. Something—*or someone*—is blocking him from moving on."

"What?" Evie blurted, her voice rising like a struck bell. "That's impossible!"

I frowned.

Excuse you, Mayor Witchy Pants, I wasn't finished.

Evie came storming toward me, dragging Jaxson with her like a stylish anchor.

Bella and Conrad followed, and for once, sweet little *Bells* looked downright pissed. She hated it when I called her that, but it never stopped me.

I couldn't remember the last time I saw her that angry. She wasn't even blinking.

"What do you mean he's stuck?" Evie asked, leaning back into Jaxson like he was a wall made just for her.

I watched, quietly surprised. My girl, the most stubborn of the three of us, was letting someone hold her up.

And more than that—*she looked stronger for it.*

Huh.

Growth.

I liked it.

Bella ran her fingers through her blonde curls like they held the answers to all our questions, while Conrad stood at her side practically vibrating.

The Python Shifter looked ready to coil up and squeeze someone if she gave the word.

And that's when it hit me.

It didn't have to be just us three Witches against the world anymore.

Maybe, *just maybe,* our Trifecta had found its match.

Three magical misfits.

Three unexpected Shifters.

A supernaturally fated support system we didn't even know we needed.

I turned back to Ryan and caught his smirk.

He knew exactly what I was thinking.

Cheeky bastard.

I shared everything I could remember from the cemetery.

Every flicker of Grandpa Al's ghost, every tremble of the earth, every whispered plea.

By the time I was done, Bella's eyes were glassy and Evie was chewing her lip like she wanted to hex someone yesterday.

"We should go to the cemetery," Jaxson said, protective instincts practically radiating from him.

Evie nodded. "I'll get Ivan."

"He'd already faded when I left," I reminded them gently. "But I get it. I'd want to check for myself, too."

The next few minutes were a whirlwind of whispered plans and hushed panic.

We were all shaken, but determined.

The party—*such as it was*—had dissolved into spell books and strategy.

Bella was already muttering incantations under her breath.

Conrad was tapping furiously into something on his enchanted tablet.

Jaxson was making lists.

We decided to reconvene in the morning, all of us needing rest—and maybe a pastry or three.

"Where should we meet?" Evie asked.

"The Tasty Tart?" I said too fast.

Ryan's grin was instant.

"Oh? And that's definitely because it's on the way to work and not because you've been depriving yourself of lattes and turnovers for days?" he whispered.

"Brat," I muttered, cheeks heating as the rest of the group started to disperse.

The cleanup was already underway.

Celeste and her date—*the one who was wearing a novelty sushi hat, because of course he was*—were waving goodnight.

Volunteers magicked away the decorations and confetti.

The firehouse was back to business and quiet in minutes.

Just me and Ryan now.

The moon was high, and the stars were doing their twinkly magic thing when we walked side by side to his truck parked outside the cemetery gates.

His shiny, royal blue pickup sparkled under the streetlamps like it belonged in a Hallmark movie featuring small-town Shifter mechanics with tragic pasts and big hands.

I kinda magicked it back for him since I didn't let him drive me earlier.

"Hop in, Honey," he murmured.

The rumble of his voice, low and intimate by my ear, sent a shiver skating down my spine. I didn't question it. I just felt it.

The rightness.

Plus, I liked his truck.

Didn't expect that.

To be fair, I didn't expect him, either.

"Wanna drive?" he asked as he opened the door for me.

I blinked. "Are you serious?"

"As a heart attack."

His grin was wicked, dimples flashing.

Holy fork.

I was smitten. Head to toe, broom to bones, starry-eyed smitten.

Without thinking twice, I reached for the lever and shoved his seat all the way back, then climbed in—right into his lap.

"I was gonna move over to the passenger side," he said, sounding more amused than shocked.

I settled in, wiggling just a little, purely for the science of it.

His hands instinctively came to rest on my hips like they belonged there.

Spoiler alert: they did.

"You work the pedals," I said, fingers curling around the steering wheel. "I'll handle the wheel."

He let out a low growl, not angry—*aroused.*

"Dangerous game, Witch."

"Yeah?" I whispered, heart hammering. "Good thing I like to play with fire."

I didn't tell him I'd stopped fighting fate.

Didn't tell him that I'd started believing in what we were.

I didn't have to.

Because with his arms around me and my hands on the wheel, we drove off together into the Castor's Corner night—*headed straight toward trouble, destiny, and maybe, just maybe, forever*—I had a feeling my big, growly, sexy as sin Bear Shifter knew.

His chest rumbled behind me, and yeah, I was positive he knew.

CHAPTER THIRTY-RYAN

I WASN'T sure what hit me harder—her flying into my lap behind the wheel of my own truck, or the ridiculous amount of joy radiating off her when she did it.

One second, I was offering to let her drive, thinking she might get a kick out of it.

The next, Donny was sitting atop my thighs, wriggling into place with a devious glint in her golden hazel eyes and announcing she'd steer while I handled the pedals.

I knew it was a terrible idea.

I also knew I wasn't saying no.

Not to her. Not ever.

Something bright and wild fluttered in my chest as I gripped the wheel and tried not to combust from the feel of her soft body bouncing on top of me with every bump in the road.

Her joy was infectious. Her laughter was pure magic. And beneath all of that?

Heat. Need. Hunger.

I felt it—*hers and mine*—rushing through the fragile bond already knitting between us.

A whisper of emotion that wasn't mine, yet lived in me anyway.

Hope. Mischief. A spark of reckless love blooming like fire.

I barely had time to process it before—BOOM—we smashed straight into one of Castor Corner's infamous moving fire hydrants.

This was one of about a dozen things on the list Conrad and I were slowly getting through, righting the wrongs the former fire chief had made.

See, Evie's idiot ex-boyfriend was the old Fire Chief, and he was an unscrupulous Wizard if ever there was one.

The idiot had magicked off the curb, then turned them invisible all because of some hair-brained scheme to increase firehouse efficiency. As if.

Anyway, neither Donny nor I had noticed the damn thing until it was too late.

She was safe, though. I made sure of that.

My arms were wrapped around her, and I cradled her precious head in my hands.

The street? Not so much.

Water exploded sky high, geysering over my freshly waxed hood like we were in a romcom gone off the rails.

"Shut up," I snarled at Jaxson, who was trying really hard not to bust a gut laughing at us from his position on his motorcycle just outside the truck.

"Who was driving?" he asked, cocking an eyebrow while he called a tow truck to hook up my ride.

"Me!" Donny and I both yelled at the same time.

Evie and Bella came running from their cars, and a few others came out of their houses too, alarmed by the splash heard 'round the block.

Conrad wasn't far behind, all wide eyes and concerned expression.

"Guess I wiggled when I should've sat still," Donny murmured, cheeks pink, lips tilted up in a grin from her antics.

My heart squeezed at the sound of her voice, and yeah, I blushed too.

I was a grown-ass Grizzly Bear Shifter with fire-fighting muscles and a culinary school diploma, and I was blushing like a teenage cub.

Donny explained what happened with a mix of sass and sheepishness, but I could tell her pride was smarting.

She didn't like being the center of a mess, even one as comical as this.

"I'll take that," I said, snagging the ticket from our friendly neighborhood Sheriff with a grunt.

Nobody was hurt, and the town insurance would cover the damage.

The only thing truly bruised was her ego—*and maybe my truck.*

"Is everyone okay?" Evie asked. "Good," she continued when we nodded, "Bella and I did a quick check, an in and out sort of thing, of the Castor mausoleum, and no sign of Grandpa Al today. So, I vote we go home, sleep on it, and start afresh tomorrow."

"Okay, sounds good," Donny replied, and nodded.

"And happy birthday, sweetie. Sorry the party got cut short," Bella said, stepping forward to hug her.

"It was great. Seriously, thank you guys," Donny said, and I could tell she wasn't lying.

They chatted a little more about their plans, but I was too busy watching my beautiful blonde Witch to pay attention to their words.

When the others finally left, I touched her arm, biting back my groan at the tingles going through me.

"Come on, I'll take you home," I said softly, anticipation and hope welling inside me.

"You sure?"

"Yes."

I squeezed her hand, grounding us both. Something deeper was brewing between us now.

She could feel it. I could feel it.

And through that whisper-thread of our bond, I felt her wondering *what now?*

At her door, I hovered behind her, drawn to the hum of her magic.

She was buzzing with emotion.

Gratitude, worry, exhaustion, affection—and something else.

Something that cracked open a space inside me that had been closed off for years.

I didn't want to crowd her, but I couldn't help nuzzling her neck.

"We'll take it one step at a time, Honey. Together."

She leaned into me like it was the most natural thing in the world.

And then we opened the door.

"Good Goddess!" I gasped.

Her familiar—*Gryn the Domovyk from hell*—was tearing through the place like a hopped-up Gremlin with a personal vendetta.

"YOU ARE DEAD, YOU SCRAWNY-BALL-SACK-HAVING-MOTHERHUMPING-ASSWIP-ING-JACKOFF-OF-A-DOMODICK!"   Donny shrieked.

Pink lightning flashed and zapped her square in the ass.

And since I had my arms wrapped around her, I got a good jolt too.

Singed me right through my jeans.

The little Hell spawn cackled and flung himself from chandelier to sofa, trashing the living room like it owed him money.

"Donny?" I said cautiously.

I could feel her magic boiling under her skin. Her rage pulsing through the bond.

She didn't answer.

She couldn't.

She was devastated.

It wasn't just about the furniture, either. I felt it. Deep down.

She was unraveling inside.

So I did the only thing I could think of—*I scooped*

her up in my arms and growled low at the furry little bastard.

"Gryn, I've spoken to Petyr," I said. "I think I understand the problem—"

"So what if you understand, Yogi? It is the *Vesterka* who must know!" he spat.

I clenched my jaw and barely resisted the urge to shift.

Just for a second.

Just to scare him.

"My Bear can only take so much disrespect when it comes to my mate," I said, letting the edge of fang show. "I'll explain it to her. But you? You. Fix. This. Mess."

"Deal," the little shit said, sniffing.

Then he vanished into a glittery puff of smugness and aftershave.

I carried Donny upstairs, still cradling her like she was the most precious thing in the world.

Because she was.

I didn't care how stubborn she was, or how hard she tried to hide her feelings.

I felt them.

Through our tiny bond.

Clear as day.

She was falling for me.

Fast.

And that was fine, because I'd already fallen for her.

Head over ass.

"Ready to talk, Honey?" I asked, nudging open the bedroom door.

Her answer knocked the wind out of me.

"Yes."

Yes?

"Yes," she repeated.

She wiggled her nose, waved her hand, then—*oh, yes, yes, yes*—she was naked.

Holy. Forking. Hell.

She stripped herself with a flick of her magic, hair tumbling around her shoulders in golden waves, curves glowing in the moonlight, and every inch of her screaming mine.

My Bear surged forward, nearly tearing free of my skin.

"Can I take your clothes off?" she whispered.

"As you wish," I growled, before our mouths met.

It was hot.

Hungry.

Intoxicating.

She didn't need to say it. I already knew.

But when she whispered again, "I'm saying yes. Yes, to everything, Ryan."

I felt the final lock click open in my chest.

"I'm gonna make you the happiest Witch in Castor's Corner, Donny Andrews," I growled."

"Good, because I'm gonna let you," she replied with that sass I loved so much.

It hit me then.

I love her.

And it was time to show her.

Kissing Donny was like biting into my favorite pastry—unexpected, addictive, and the kind of indulgence that ruins you for anything else.

Sweet and spicy, bold and soft, magic and mayhem wrapped in a body that made my Bear roll over and show his belly.

She wasn't just a woman. She was my woman. And tonight, after all the resisting, the hiding, the second guessing—*she was finally mine.*

I'd already carried her upstairs like a prize, though really, I was the one who'd won.

Gently, I laid her down on the bed—*our bed now*—and wasn't that kismet? I knew it to the marrow of my bones.

Donatella Andrews was it for me. The beginning and the end.

She leaned back on her elbows, bare legs open and inviting, golden hair tousled from my touch, lips swollen from our kisses, and those wicked, clever eyes on me like she knew exactly what I was about to do to her. And hell yes, she did.

I knelt between her thighs, palms bracing on either side of her hips, not touching her yet.

Just looking. Memorizing. Revering.

My Bear rumbled low in my chest, urging me forward.

"This isn't one night, Honey," I told her, my voice thick with all the emotion I didn't know how to name. "This is forever. Tell me you understand. Tell me you want it."

She didn't hesitate. Donny arched her back, pressing those full, perfect breasts into my hands, and I nearly lost it right there.

My mouth descended like a man starved. I licked a trail across the warm swell of her breasts, circling each nipple with slow, deliberate attention before drawing one between my lips.

Her whimpers undid me. Her thighs quivered against my ribs. I could feel the heat of her arousal soaking through her folds, scenting the air like magic and sex and everything holy.

"Tell me," I growled again when she reached for my hand, trying to guide me lower.

I needed to hear it this time. No more dancing around what we were. I needed the words.

"This isn't a one-night thing," she said, breathless but certain. "This is the start of our forever, Ryan. I'm ready now. Ready for you to claim me, mate."

Mate.

I reared back, needing to see her face as she said it.

Her lips curved into a smile, her fingers caressing my cheek.

"Fuck yes, I'm gonna claim you, Honey," I growled, grabbing my cock and guiding the thick head to her slick entrance. "Mine."

I pushed inside.

Inch by inch.

Tight, hot, perfect.

She gasped, her eyes wide as I filled her completely, and I knew right then I'd never get over this feeling. I didn't want to.

"Oh Goddess, you're so deep," she whimpered, and my Bear preened like he'd just caught the biggest salmon in the stream.

I cradled her face and kissed her, soft and reverent, like the sacred act this was.

Our bodies rocked together in perfect rhythm.

Every moan, every movement felt like it had always been meant to happen.

But then she gripped my ass with both hands and gave it a firm, possessive slap.

"You don't have to treat me like I'm glass, Bear Boy," she growled. "I'm a Witch, and you can fuck me like I know you want to."

Her magic zapped my ass for emphasis.

Holy hell.

I snarled and obeyed.

Thrust after thrust, I drove into her with the hunger I'd been holding back for far too long.

"Good mate," I groaned. "So perfect. Made for me."

My fangs extended, my Bear riding just under the surface as we climbed higher.

I could feel her magic wrapping around us, shimmering along my skin like stardust. I bent her knees, hit that deep spot inside her, and watched her come undone.

"Ryan! Please!" she cried out, her body clenching tight.

I flipped us, holding her above me, letting her ride.

Her nails scored my chest, and I bared my throat to her in offering.

She kissed me instead, but when she leaned her head back and exposed her own throat, I knew. It was time.

My fangs pierced her skin, right over the pulse that beat for me, and I sank into her in every way a Shifter could.

My mate.

She screamed my name, her orgasm hitting hard, magic crashing into mine.

It felt like lightning.

Like coming home.

Like the whole damn universe had been holding its breath, waiting for this moment.

We weren't two people anymore.

We were one.

Marked. Mated. Bound.

The rest of the night blurred into a frenzy of pleasure and claiming, whispered *I love yous*, and sweet, aching touches.

I made her come until she couldn't say my name anymore.

Until the sun began to rise and her head rested on my chest with a soft, sleepy sigh.

She was mine now.

And I was so fucking hers.

Forever.

Our bond ignited, sealing what fate had already written.

And when she curled against me afterwards, soft and sweet and sated, I heard her last thought before she drifted off.

I'm yours.

Yeah, Honey.

You're mine, too.

And I was.

Forever.

CHAPTER THIRTY-ONE-DONNY

I WOKE up to the most forking divine smell to ever exist.

Like the Goddess herself had turned my house into a five-star bakery.

Cherry pie filling.

White chocolate ganache.

Devil's food cookies.

Blueberry scones.

Buttery croissants.

And—*oh sweet cauldrons of caffeine*—coffee.

Fresh, strong, sinful coffee.

I sat bolt upright, my senses on high alert.

What sorcery was this?

One deep inhale and I practically levitated out of bed. I didn't even care about my hair.

For the first time since that rotten little Domovyk turned me into a magical Barbie, I didn't curse the sight of my golden locks in the mirror.

In fact, with the leftover pink flush from beard burn and that post-mating glow, I looked kinda cute.

"Hot damn," I whispered to myself, fluffing my curls. "Maybe being mated to a Bear Shifter with pastry fingers is the key to eternal beauty."

I slipped into a pleated Marina Rinaldi dress—*flowy, flattering, and kind to my very recently well-used thighs*—and padded downstairs, bare feet light on the wood floors.

Then I froze.

My jaw dropped.

My entire house was *perfect*.

Like, forking magazine-spread-level perfect.

Not a single broken vase.

Not one stuffing-stripped cushion.

The walls had been patched, the floors mopped, the picture frames re-hung. It was like Gryn had never had a furniture-destroying temper tantrum.

Or pooped in my Uggs.

I crept toward the kitchen and stopped in my tracks again.

There he was.

The devil himself.

Gryn, my furry, foul-mouthed, chaos-gremlin of a familiar, perched on a barstool like he hadn't wrecked my home just twelve hours earlier.

He was polishing off what looked like a tray of scones the size of dinner plates and sipping from a comically large coffee mug that read *World's Grumpiest HouseGod*.

"Good morning, *Vesterka*," he said with a buttery grin, licking crumbs off his stubby fingers. "Sleep well?"

"Are you—did you—what?" I spluttered as if my brain had short-circuited.

"What? Is my beard on backwards?" Gryn quirked a brow. "Maybe you give me a trim later? I will call the blue-haired one. She books fast."

Before I could gather a single coherent thought, the back door creaked open and in walked my Bear.

My big, beautiful Bear.

Ryan, dressed in a clingy tee and sweatpants, holding sprigs of rosemary like he'd just returned from a sexy woodland forage.

His hair was tousled, his eyes soft, and that kiss he dropped on me?

Good Goddess, it shorted my circuits for a whole different reason.

"Move in with me?" I blurted.

His brows lifted slightly.

"I wasn't going to assume, but are you sure, Honey?"

I nodded, heart racing.

"Yep."

"Because I recall having to wait weeks for you to even notice me," he teased, lifting a cherry turnover to my lips.

I held out, just barely.

"I won't eat it until you answer."

Ryan grinned, all cocky and smug in the way that made my ovaries throw confetti.

"Also, the longer you make me wait now, the more revenge I'm taking later in the bedroom," I warned. "And I do mean revenge."

He leaned closer, lips brushing mine.

"Yes, you silly Witch. Of course I'm moving in. You're mine now."

Cherry filling be damned, I melted right there in his arms.

We kissed like lovers with all the time in the world, and I tasted sugar and heat and something that felt an awful lot like forever.

The kitchen faded away as I ended up on Ryan's lap, alternating between coffee sips and pastry bites while he fed me like I was the queen of the freaking forest.

We talked about everything and nothing, easy as breathing. It felt good.

Grounded.

Like maybe, *just maybe*, this wild life of mine was finally starting to settle in the right direction.

Until the Bear had to open his big, beautiful mouth.

"One thing," Ryan said, brushing crumbs from my cheek.

I stilled. "What?"

"Well, Honey, about Gryn. See, Domovyks used to be gods."

"Come again?"

"Minor household gods. But yeah. Worshiped, powerful, demanding. You know how it is."

"No, I do not know how it is, Ryan. Because I did not get a how-to manual on handling magical household Gremlins."

He chuckled, unbothered by my rising tone. "Basically, Gryn expects tribute."

"Tribute," I echoed, blinking.

"Yeah. Like food. Trinkets. Milk."

"Milk?! He dumped in my vintage Guccis, and now he wants *MILK*?"

Ryan was smiling like a man in love and also slightly afraid for his life.

"I'll take care of it, Honey. I'll do the cooking. I'll leave him his offerings. No need to stress. I just wanted you to know why he's been behaving like—um."

"Like he was raised by evil Trolls?"

"Right. Anyway, would that be okay with you?"

"Would what be okay? Oh, you mean you cooking and providing him with his milk? Heck yeah! Thank the *fu-forking* Goddess," I breathed, slumping against him.

"You almost said it," he whispered, licking my ear.

"Said what?"

"Fork. You almost dropped a real F-bomb."

"I am trying, okay? The pink lightning stings like heck."

Ryan kissed the top of my head.

"Well, try harder, because the last time you said it, we both got zapped. And I'm not looking to run out of pants."

He grinned. I giggled. But I promised.

Then, we made out on the kitchen chair like teenagers until I glanced at the clock.

"Thirty-three minutes till my first client," I muttered.

"Hmm," Ryan hummed, lifting me by the waist and adjusting the hem of my dress.

He slipped a hand under the fabric, fingers trailing along my inner thigh until they found what they were looking for.

I gasped. "Ryan!"

"Plenty of time, Honey."

I couldn't argue.

Not with that grin.

Not with those hands.

Not when he was mine—and I was his.

And as he kissed me senseless right there in the kitchen, the smell of coffee and sugar lingering in the air, I realized something.

This?

This was home.

Forking finally.

CHAPTER THIRTY-TWO-DONNY

MY LEGS LOCKED around his waist the second his arms banded around me, and then—*BAM*—we were moving. No, flying.

Ryan tore through the house with inhuman speed, carrying me like a prize he'd fought a thousand battles to win.

And maybe he had.

We landed in my—*no, our*—bedroom in a blur of magic and desire, his mouth crashing down on mine like I was air and he'd been suffocating.

When he pulled back, his dark eyes gleamed with hunger and affection, and he grinned like the damn cat that caught the canary—*and then built a bakery just to feed it pastries and pet it every morning.*

"You're mine now, Honey," he growled.

Oh, fork me, I loved the sound of that.

Before I could snark something back—*maybe a quip about collars or claiming*—his callused hands slipped under my dress and up my thighs, rough fingers grazing over silky skin and making me arch like a spell-struck hussy.

The skirt bunched at my waist, and then his shoulders nudged between my legs, forcing them open wide as he settled in like he was home.

Because he was. Right there. Between my thighs.

On his knees.

In my bed.

With that look in his eyes like I was his Goddess-damned religion.

I propped myself up on my elbows just in time to see his wicked tongue lick a path over my lace panties—from one hole to the other.

Oh, sweet steaming lattes.

I nearly combusted.

He sucked and licked like a man on a mission, the friction of the fabric against my sensitive flesh dragging sharp moans from my throat.

"Ryan—"

I tried to speak, to plead, to curse—but all that came out was a strangled sob of please.

As I tumbled into bliss, he growled low in his

throat, lifting himself onto his knees and pushing my panties aside with reverent urgency.

My eyes went wide when I saw his cock, thick and throbbing, nestled in his big hand.

And then—*sweet moon above*—he was pressing inside, inch by impossible inch.

Stretching me. Claiming me. Filling me in a way no spell, no curse, no fantasy ever could.

And for the next eleven and a half minutes, Ryan McLeod proved it—thrust by delicious thrust, until my soul felt branded and my body hummed with the kind of afterglow that could power half of Castor's Corner.

"Love you, my beautiful blonde Witch," he said, his voice thick with emotion and need.

"I love you too, mate."

And then I think I blacked out for a few moments.

But when I opened my eyes again, there he was, taking care of me, and I just knew I was one lucky Witch.

I finally had my happy ever after.

And he was better than I dreamed.

CHAPTER THIRTY-THREE-DONNY

I ARRIVED AT HAIR NOW, Gone Tomorrow only ten minutes late.

That was on me.

Well, mostly on me.

I'd been the one to beg for seconds.

And thirds.

And a side of Bear growling with extra whipped cream.

I was fully sated but walking like I'd just ridden a mechanical bull after a wine tasting.

Celeste arched a brow the moment I limped through the door.

"You alright? Did Gryn do something to your closet again?" she asked, taking in my outfit with a puzzled expression.

I looked down and—*sweet tartlets of terror*—I was wearing pale pink pants and a baby blue blouse.

I looked like a sad cotton candy cone melting in the sun.

"Holy forking crappuccinos!"

"No worries. I got this." Celeste twirled her fingers, and a warm shimmer of magic flowed over me.

The pastel nightmare faded, replaced by rich mocha tones and golden accents that actually worked with my hair.

Like fall had exploded on me—*in a good way.*

"Thanks," I muttered, smoothing the long tunic over my hips and slipping behind the front desk. "Where's my first appointment?"

Celeste bit her lip. Uh-oh.

"Oh, uh, they canceled," she said quietly.

"Canceled?" I echoed. "Did they say why?"

She shook her head.

Weird. No one ever canceled on me.

I was the stylist in Castor's Corner.

People waited six moons and three eclipses to book with me. I didn't even do kids' cuts unless they were related to the Mayor.

Something prickled at the base of my neck.

A tingle that had nothing to do with hair or

fashion or even my incredibly sore, incredibly satisfied lady parts.

No. This was magic.

The bad kind.

I dropped into my seat, suddenly wide awake. With Gryn acting civil, Grandpa Al stuck in some kind of spiritual purgatory, and mysterious clients canceling out of the blue?

Something was coming.

And I'd need every bit of power—*and pastry-fueled support*—to deal with it.

But first?

I sipped the coffee Ryan had brewed and left for me in a thermos wrapped in a note that read:

Love you, Honey. Kick ass today.
-Ryan

I smiled. I could do that.

Sometime later.

Celeste hung up the phone with a soft sigh that sounded like defeat.

I didn't have to ask.

I already knew.

My heart sank like a stone in a bubbling cauldron.

That was the sixth cancellation in under ten minutes.

"What the actual fork is happening?" I muttered, staring at my color-coded appointment book that was slowly bleeding red ink like it had sprung a leak in the space-time continuum.

My hands were shaking.

Not from rage.

Not even from panic.

From heartbreak.

This place—*Hair Now, Gone Tomorrow*—was more than a salon.

It was my legacy. My sanctuary.

The one damn thing I'd built with my own magic-stained hands. And now, it was unraveling in real-time like some kind of slow-motion hex.

"Donny!" Evie's voice rang out like a bell, jolting me back to the present.

She was waving something wildly in her hand and barreling through the front door like a woman possessed.

"Look!" she gasped, breathless, shoving the paper in my face.

My fingers trembled as I snatched it. One glance and I felt the blood drain from my body.

It was a flyer.

Cheap paper.

Bad font.

And an even worse photo.

Henry the Hedgehog's haircut—*but mangled.*

Violated.

Someone had gone over it with what looked like a damn weed whacker.

His soft spines were lopsided, jagged, and uneven, like he'd lost a bar fight with a rabid garden gnome.

Below the photo, bold black letters screamed across the page. The message was clear:

If you want to wind up bald, go to Hair Now, Gone Tomorrow, where the salon owner doesn't care if she shaves your head and leaves you looking like hex victim!

"I didn't do that to Henry!" I cried out, clutching the flyer to my chest like I could absorb the lie and strangle it to death.

Bella burst through the door next, bless her sugar-dusted soul, holding a pastry box like it was a life raft.

"Mrs. Fox brought that to me," Evie said solemnly, nodding at the flyer. "But first, Bella brought reinforcements."

"Here, have a Pumpkin Fudge Delight. You look like you're about to eat someone," Bella whispered.

She wasn't wrong.

I yanked open the box, shoved two glorious pieces of pumpkin-chocolate magic into my mouth, and chewed like my life depended on it.

Fudge and spice flooded my senses, grounding me. The tears prickling my eyes receded a bit.

"Oh, the texture," I moaned around the sugary mass. "The cinnamon. The blessed fork-tastic after burn."

Celeste sidled closer, eyeing the box.

I growled low in my throat, snatched a third piece, then shoved the remains at her.

"Better?" Bella asked dryly, clearly unfazed by my emotional eating spiral.

"Yeah," I grunted. "I'm good. Thanks."

"Honey!" Ryan's voice boomed through the doorway a heartbeat later.

He stormed in, followed by Jaxson and Conrad.

Each of them held a different flyer in their hands.

More accusations.

More lies.

"This one says the crematorium failed inspection," Jaxson growled.

"And this one says you've got rats," Conrad added with a deadly frown.

Celeste gasped beside me, holding her flyer like it was dipped in poison.

"Someone's trying to ruin you, Donny. This is a coordinated attack."

No shit, Sherlock.

I wanted to scream, cry, zap someone into a new hair dimension and back.

I wanted answers. But more than anything, I wanted to know why? *Why me?*

Hair and magic were my things.

I wasn't trying to be queen of the coven or start turf wars. I just wanted to make people feel beautiful and maybe charm their highlights to last six weeks longer.

Now, thanks to some malicious mystery menace, I was on the brink of losing it all.

And still, my people showed up for me.

Bella gave my hand a tight squeeze before marching outside, shouting something about a location spell and rounding up every flyer in a five-mile radius.

Conrad followed her like a silent, scaly guard dog.

Evie gave me a hug that felt like a warm blanket

and whispered she'd follow up with Ivan about Grandpa Al.

And Ryan?

Ryan didn't say much. He just stood behind me, his massive chest radiating calm and protection, one hand on my shoulder like a grounding tether.

When the last call came in—*another cancellation*—I closed my book.

Red lines slashed through every appointment like angry scars.

"This isn't a fluke," I whispered. "Someone is out to destroy me."

"But they won't succeed," Ryan said, low and sure.

I nodded, swallowing the lump in my throat.

"No. They won't. But I need to regroup."

I turned to Celeste.

"Close up. I'm going home. You'll get two weeks' pay, but I can't promise anything past that."

"Donny—" she started.

"Don't. It's okay," I interrupted gently. "I'm going to fix this. Somehow."

Evie and Jaxson left after another round of hugs. I locked the doors to my salon with trembling fingers, feeling the weight of my magical lineage press on my shoulders like a crown I hadn't realized I was wearing.

"We'll get to the bottom of this," Ryan said again as he helped me into the truck.

I nodded, unable to speak.

My magic was buzzing, irritated and raw, sparking along my skin in angry flickers.

I curled up in my seat, cradling my hands in my lap.

I wasn't weak.

I wasn't broken.

But Gaia help whoever thought they could take me down without a fight.

"Home?" he asked softly.

"Yeah. I need a bath. And maybe a glass of wine the size of my head."

"I'll start dinner," he said, kissing the back of my hand. "And we'll figure out the rest together."

He held my hand the whole ride back.

Said nothing else. Just let me exist.

He really was the best of men—and Bears.

I was one lucky Witch. I knew that.

And he was lucky, too. I mean, at my core I was a good person. I knew that too.

I just wished I didn't have to come with a side of trouble.

Goddess, I was such a mess.

"Hey, you're my mess, Honey, and I wouldn't want you any other way," Ryan said, kindness and humor lighting his warm eyes.

I loved the way he read my mind. And even more, I loved the way he loved me.

When we pulled into the driveway, I stared at my —*our*—little house like it was the last piece of solid ground in a storm.

Ryan opened the door, lifted me down like I was made of spun sugar and firelight, and looked into my eyes like I was still worth something even if the whole world had turned against me.

"Hungry?" he asked, his voice warm.

"For you," I whispered.

Because yeah. I had things to fix.

Spells to cast.

Lies to destroy.

But first?

I needed my mate.

Wanted my big, strong Bear to make me feel good.

I was thinking a long, hot soak in a tub with him in it was just what this Witch ordered.

Let the world try to tear me down. I wasn't done yet.

Not by a long shot.

CHAPTER THIRTY-FOUR
DONNY

THE DAYS WERE BLURRING TOGETHER like a watercolor left out in the rain.

I'd spent most of them curled up in bed, watching the golden Autumn light shift across the walls while the rest of Castor's Corner prepared for the big Halloween Bash.

Normally, this time of year would have been my busiest—updos, color refreshes, supernatural glam squads on speed dial.

But my salon sat empty.

My appointment book looked like a barren wasteland.

I'd even caught sight of some very unfortunate bangs wandering around town like lost souls.

Bangs I didn't cut, mind you.

That would've been too much to bear.

And yet here I was.

A Witch with a glittering matebond, a house that finally felt like a home again, and the most perfect Bear Shifter boyfriend-slash-live-in-lover-slash-breakfast god anyone could dream up.

I should've been doing cartwheels through the moonlight.

Instead, I was a walking ball of guilt and inertia.

Ryan had officially moved in, and if there were a class on how to be the most attentive, devoted, toe-curling mate in the world, he could teach it blindfolded.

I adored him.

I loved waking up tangled in his arms, sneaking steamy kisses between his bakery shifts, and falling asleep to the sound of his bear-sized snores.

But the joy was laced with something else now.

A knot of shame I couldn't seem to untangle.

"I'll see ya later, Honey. I've got the early shift at the bakery," Ryan murmured as he leaned down to kiss me awake.

His lips were warm, tasting faintly of cinnamon and sleepy devotion.

"Love you," I replied softly, nuzzling into his chest.

"I love you too, Donatella."

He winked at me, pulled the blanket back up to my chin like I was made of spun sugar, and was gone in a swirl of flannel and oven-bound purpose.

And what was I doing?

Hiding under a blanket fort with my hair in a scrunchie that hadn't seen daylight in three days.

I was an emotional Waffle House. Open, but barely functioning. And mostly, not good for anyone.

I sighed and pulled the covers over my head again.

What else did I have to do?

Every spell I'd tried to help Grandpa Al cross over fizzled out like old soda.

Our seance attempt had been a bust.

No ghostly whispers.

No magical sparkles.

Just me, Evie, and Bella sitting around a table with tea lights and zero results.

I felt useless.

And I hated it.

I was just sinking deeper into my self-pity pit, contemplating whether I should go full recluse and live among the squirrels, when suddenly—*BANG!*

The bedroom doors burst open with all the

subtlety of a wrecking ball, and then—

"YAAAAAAH!"

A hairy, cranky, two-and-a-half-foot-tall missile launched itself at my bed.

"GYAAH—GRYN?!"

Before I could react, the covers were torn off me like I was the main course at a magic-infused intervention, and there stood the newly rejuvenated Domovyk—*his fur fluffed to perfection, eyes glowing with righteous fury, and his little hands planted on his hips like an angry Soviet auntie.*

"DONATELLA ANDREWS," he bellowed in a voice that quite literally made the entire house shake, "IT IS TIME TO PUT ON YOUR BIG GIRL PANTS AND GET OUT OF THIS BED!"

I blinked, stunned. "Um. Excuse me?"

"You are acting like you have been beaten," Gryn growled, eyes narrowing. "When you have not even FOUGHT."

"I have fought," I mumbled.

"You sulked. You cried. You rewatched every season of Buffy. Thrice! Now get up! And for the love of the Goddess, brush your teeth! TODAY—" he raised his tiny arms, lightning crackling from his fingers like a pissed-off Pikachu "—WE GO TO WAR!"

Then he zapped me.

ZAPPED. ME.

A bolt of pure Domovyk magic hit me square in the stomach, and I screamed—but not in pain.

Oh no.

I screamed because I was suddenly airborne, wrapped in my top sheet like a flying burrito, and hurled into my own shower stall like a high-speed cannonball of Witchy doom.

SLAM. SPLASH.

The water turned on by itself.

Yep, it really did.

Gryn stomped to the edge of the bathroom and shouted over the sound of the water, "Be clean. Be proud. Be dangerous."

And then he was gone.

I just sat there in the stall, soaking wet, dripping and stunned for full ten seconds. Before I started laughing.

I laughed so hard I wheezed.

That little hairy menace had just shock-launched me back into functioning.

And you know what?

He was right.

I wasn't done yet. Not by a long shot.

Someone had come for my livelihood. They tried

to take my reputation, my clients, my confidence. But they forgot one very important detail.

I was a Castor's Corner Witch.

And now?

I had a mate, a houseful of magic, and a damn Domovyk ready to go full mystical mafia on my behalf.

So yeah. I'd start with clean hair and brushed teeth.

And then?

Then I'd remind this town exactly who the fork they were messing with.

CHAPTER THIRTY-FIVE—GRYN

A FEW MINUTES EARLIER.

Ahhh, the scent of toasted almonds and pumpkin fudge still clung to my whiskers.

Divine. Absolutely divine.

The Bear had done it again.

Tributes were being paid. At last.

Proper meals.

A designated sunbeam for napping.

Even belly rubs when I permitted them.

And my Witch? My Witch was glowing—though she didn't know it yet.

Still licking her wounds, poor pitiful thing.

But that would change. Oh yes.

Because I had plan.

A glorious, diabolical, brilliant plan!

I scurried into the kitchen and leapt onto the counter with a somersault that would've made my Uncle Grizzle proud (he was eaten by a rabid kitchen Gnome in 1432 but had impeccable form).

With a flick of my claws, I rolled out the enchanted parchment I'd borrowed permanently from the Council of Familiars.

It glowed in eerie, shimmering ink as I tapped it dramatically.

"Operation HAG WRATH."

"Phase One," I said to the room (and to the raccoon watching through the window—I suspected he was a spy), "Identify the Enemy."

A series of tiny sketches danced across the parchment.

Suspicious townsfolk with grumpy faces, uneven haircuts, and a deep, irrational hatred of well-run magical salons. Hmm.

"Phase Two: Misinformation Assault." I hissed and flicked a drop of honey onto the page.

Instantly, the paper showed hundreds of miniature flyers swirling into flames, screaming like tiny banshees.

Gryn 1, Salon Saboteurs 0.

"Phase Three..." My voice dropped low,

dramatic, shaking with vengeance and fondness and —*dare I say*—love.

"Rebuild. Reclaim. REIGN."

I stared at Donatella's name scrawled in golden ink at the top of the page and let out a sigh so heartfelt it startled the raccoon, who fell backward into the trash.

She was mine.

My Witch.

My sacred charge.

And I would not rest until every saboteur in Castor's Corner was hexed, humbled, and possibly given a bad dye job for the next seven generations.

"They want war?" I snarled, leaping off the counter with a twirl of my tail and landing squarely in a bowl of glitter.

"They've got war. And this time, the Familiar bites back."

Then I was off to get my Witchy moving.

CHAPTER THIRTY-SIX-DONNY

LATER THAT SAME DAY.

"Gryn, I've been to the cemetery every single day since Grandpa Al first showed up to me, and I haven't seen a ghostly hair or heard a single spectral sigh since," I muttered, hugging myself.

"Because you have not returned alone," Gryn sniffed.

"I am still not alone!" I snapped, immediately regretting how petulant I sounded.

Like some baby Witch who lost her wand at daycare. Ugh.

"I am not other," Gryn said, his voice low and resonant. "I am an extension of you, as your *familiar*. Now, lead the way to the grave."

He gestured like he was inviting me into battle, not a graveyard.

Dramatic little fuzzball.

"Um, Gryn? When we're done, do you think you could do a line from Terminator for me?" I asked, because honestly, his accent would slay with a *"I'll be back."*

"I am not Austrian," he grumbled. "And this is no joke."

But I caught it—the tiniest twitch at the corner of his grumpy little mouth.

Ha. Victory.

He'd never admit it, but he was warming up to me. And not just because of my Bear's scones.

Finally.

I should also mention said scones were amazeballs.

All puns intended.

Snort. Chortle.

Focus, Donny.

We walked in silence toward the cemetery, our shoes crunching over fallen leaves in glorious shades of pumpkin, paprika, and caramel.

Castor's Corner was absolutely dripping with Autumn, and it would've been dreamy if not for the fact that I was basically a pariah.

People avoided my gaze like I was the literal plague.

The very same people I'd pampered, highlighted, and glamorized for years now couldn't even muster a polite hello.

My gut twisted.

My salon was a ghost town, and it wasn't just business—*it was my magic, my pride, my calling.*

But the kicker? Half these Witches were walking around with brassy roots, patchy dye jobs, and tragic man buns.

Like please. Have some dignity.

I smiled tightly at a few familiar faces, but not one met my eyes.

"When we arrive, *Vesterka*," Gryn said, his tone reverent, "you must allow your insight to guide you. I have called Ivan and Petyr. Your Trifecta is on the way. But there is something you must do first."

I groaned but nodded. I couldn't shake the feeling that I was at the edge of something bigger than I was ready for—*but also something I had to face.*

Then a zap stung my left butt cheek.

"Goddess! I didn't even curse that time!" I yelped, rubbing my rear.

"Stop taunting the divine," Gryn said primly,

pointing ahead like the world's sassiest, furriest tour guide.

Reluctantly, I stepped off the path, following my intuition toward the Castorini Mausoleum.

My outfit of the day—a Tom Ford satin ombré blouse-and-wide-leg-pants combo—billowed around me like enchanted leaves.

I was fall fabulous and refusing to hide from the world, even if the world had decided to blacklist me.

I hummed under my breath, letting my magic swell inside me like a tide. With every step, the sensation grew stronger.

Warmer.

Like something inside me had finally clicked back into place. My fingers tingled, my chest lifted, and for the first time in days, I felt like me again.

Powerful. Purposeful. Ready.

"That's it, *Vesterka*," Gryn whispered behind me. "So close to what you are meant for."

I turned to thank him—*just in time to see he'd stopped walking, his big eyes fixed on me like a proud little battle general.*

Then I noticed it.

Nestled behind the mausoleum, half-buried in fallen leaves and moss, was a circle of jagged stones.

The energy coming off it made my stomach clench.

"Is that a circle?" I asked, pointing.

A low moan echoed through the air, and suddenly the mausoleum shimmered with swirling black smoke.

Then he appeared.

Grandpa Al.

Same sorrowful eyes.

Same gaping ghostly groin wound.

Still dead. Still stuck. And still sad.

My heart squeezed.

"Donatella? You've returned to help me? I thought you had decided I was not worthy," he said mournfully, fading in and out of view.

My chest ached. "No, Grandpa. No. I've been back—every day. But I wasn't alone, and I guess that blocked you from reaching me."

"I see, ragazza. You tried. Just please tell Evie and Bella I'm sorry I didn't say goodbye. And sorrier still, I won't be able to see you in the Next Amazing Journey."

"No! Wait—don't fade! Look, I found this!" I pointed desperately to the circle of rocks.

The second I got closer, nausea rolled through me like a wave.

My magic recoiled instinctively.

"What, Vesterka? It's a Ghost-repelling circle, no?"

I shook my head.

No, this wasn't the typical graveyard circle of stones.

There was something wrong with this spell. Anchored in hate, in fear, in petty vengeance.

It was dark magic. Designed to repel? Yes. Like a traditional banishment ward. But something was off.

I searched the ether, pulling on all my knowledge and instincts as I tried to get a read on what this circle of stones was for. And when it hit me, it hit hard.

"This isn't here to banish the dead from the cemetery. It's to trap a soul in limbo."

"Don't touch it yet," Gryn barked. "You must understand what it is first."

Grandpa Al clutched his chest, groaning. "So much hate, it burns me. Donatella, you must not face this alone. Call your cousins. They will help—"

"No," I said, voice shaking. "I got this."

The magic in me swelled, golden and wild, and I dropped to my knees in the grass.

I didn't know who cast this spell.

I didn't know why.

But I knew one thing for sure.

No one was going to take my family from me.

Alive or dead.

Not this time.

Not ever.

CHAPTER THIRTY-SEVEN- RYAN

THE SMELL of rising dough and roasted cinnamon filled the air, warm and comforting.

Normally, the steady rhythm of bakery work helped clear my head.

Mixing, kneading, baking—*there was peace in the routine.*

But not today.

Today, the batter was perfect, the pastries golden, and still I couldn't stop thinking about Donny.

She'd been quiet all morning, withdrawn ever since the truth about those damn flyers came out.

The salon—her pride, her place—targeted by people who didn't deserve to shine her boots.

It made my teeth ache to think about how much that place meant to her.

How hard she'd worked.

How much of herself she poured into every snip of the scissors.

And now, someone was trying to destroy it. And for what?

I pressed the heel of my hand into a mound of dough, wishing it were the face of whoever was behind this.

"She deserves better," I muttered to myself.

"Hmm?" Bella called over her shoulder as she boxed up a batch of ghost-shaped donuts.

"Nothing," I said. "Just thinking."

Thinking of my mate.

Of how she kissed me with her whole heart, even when she pretended to push me away.

Of how she muttered threats to her grumpy familiar like a sailor but cried in secret over every lost client.

Of how she kissed my fingertips like they were sacred.

My mate. My Witch. My Donatella.

My chest tightened.

And then—it hit me.

A tug.

Not physical, not visible, but deeper than nerves, deeper than breath.

The matebond.

It yanked tight, sudden and sharp, like a fishhook snagging my sternum.

I froze, one flour-covered hand in midair.

"Donny."

Something was wrong.

My blood turned cold. I turned toward Bella, who was staring at her phone with wide eyes.

"Bella?" I growled.

She held up the screen, her face paling. "Gryn just texted me."

I crossed the counter in a blink, reading the words.

GRYN

Something is wrong with Grandpa Al.
Donny needs help. Now.

My Bear surged forward, half-shift clawing at my skin, ready to destroy whoever had dared hurt what was mine.

"Where is she?" I asked, barely controlling the rumble in my throat.

Bella shoved off her apron. "I don't know, but I think they went to the cemetery—Gryn was talking to Petyr about dark magic and Grandpa Al yesterday."

I was already moving. "Let's go."

Bella raced beside me, grabbing her bag. "Evie's on her way. We'll meet them there."

I didn't stop to grab my jacket. Didn't care that I had flour in my hair or dough on my jeans.

I just knew my mate needed me.

"Hang on, Honey," I growled, pushing the door open with one flour-dusted hand. "I'm coming for you."

CHAPTER THIRTY-EIGHT-DONNY

JUST AS I got close to the stones, the sound of persons familiar to me stopped me in my tracks.

"What are—"

"—you doing?"

"Get away from that!"

Their twin voices came from the left, oily and sharp like a hex gone wrong.

My head snapped toward the woods where Candice and Denice Chickazola, former owners of my salon and occasional root touch-up disasters, emerged from the trees like low-budget Halloween villains.

Their outfits were identical—pumpkin-orange sacks that looked like someone had wrapped them in party streamers and glue sticks.

And their hair? Great Aunt Edna's bunions, their heads were a travesty.

Crooked home-done dye jobs, half-scorched strands sticking out in tufts, one of them rocking a faux hawk that would've made Johnny Rotten weep.

They looked like the love children of a scarecrow and a punk rock nightmare.

I was too stunned to speak, and it got worse.

Grandpa Al, still hovering ghost-pale and hole-in-the-middle, groaned.

"The Chicky twins? You're still alive?"

"Grandpa Al!" I gasped, appalled.

"You had to say that?" I hissed at him. "They already look like they crawled out of a cauldron backwards."

"Yes, handsome Al," Denice purred, her gravelly voice somehow both flirtatious and furious, hands on her nonexistent hips.

"—we are still alive. And we're waiting for you to keep—"

"—your promise!" Candice finished with a pout that would've been cute if it weren't laced with psychotic intent.

"We found out about your two-timing ways, Al," Denice snarled.

"—and that was not nice!"

Al floated backward. "Beautiful ladies, I-I didn't realize we were exclusive! It was just a bit of harmless fun!"

"Harmless?" they both shrieked. "We mourned you for years!"

"And now we've bound you to this place—"

"—to suffer as we have!"

A flash of power cracked the circle of stones at my feet.

Grandpa Al howled, his translucent form sparking and fading. My gut twisted.

Holy fork. His ghost nuts were being flash-fried.

And maybe, sure, maybe the old horndog deserved a little comeuppance. But this?

This was soul death. And for what—*some over-the-hill grudge sex?*

"Stop it!" I shouted, stepping forward even as the ground trembled under a new pulse of dark energy.

I flicked a look to Gryn, who stood quietly like a furry little general, waiting for my command.

"You can't do this to him! It's wrong. You're not just binding him—you're unraveling his very soul!"

Candice raised a gnarled brow. "So what?"

"Yeah," Denice added with a venomous smirk. "You can't stop us. You're just a hairstylist."

"Are you even that anymore?" Candice mocked. "Seems like you've lost a few clients."

My chest cracked. My fists curled.

"You?" I whispered. "You're behind those flyers?"

"Of course!" Denice bragged.

"You started poking around here—"

"—so we gave you something else to worry about."

Petty. Vindictive. Cruel.

I almost hoped the Goddess would let me curse, just this once. But I held it in, barely.

"You're attacking my business? Ruining my reputation? All to torture a Ghost because your mutual booty call never promised you a magical white wedding?"

"Al never promised either of you anything, did he?" I pressed, watching the flicker of hesitation behind their over-plucked brows.

Silence. Guilt. Bingo.

"And now you want vengeance because you regret it? Grow up."

Evie, Bella, Jaxson, Conrad, and Ryan arrived just as I turned to Grandpa Al, who was flickering like a dying candle.

"Hold on, old man."

Bella gasped. "Grandpa Al!"

"Stop this, please," Evie pleaded with the twins.

"Never!" they cried in unison. "No one uses the Chicky twins!"

"Donny?" Ryan's voice snapped my attention to the stone circle again.

I knew what I had to do. It was risky, reckless, borderline stupid—*but it was right.*

I whispered a prayer to the Goddess.

Protection.

Clarity.

No zaps to the butt, please.

Then I summoned my magic, unfiltered and fierce, and spoke the spell from somewhere deep inside.

"Goddess be fair,

I've cleaned up my chat,

Please give me a bolster,

To end this fake tit for tat.

The Chickys are wrong,

They deserve no reprisals,

Young love made willingly,

Now turned into rivals.

Help me survive while,

I stop this bad curse,

You are all powerful,

Don't do your worst."

Hey, it wasn't Shakespeare.

But I didn't say the F word, and that had to earn me points.

With a deep breath and a heart full of chaotic Gryffindor-esque energy, I dropped to my knees and shoved my hand straight into the cursed circle.

Agony. Searing, electric, reality-bending pain jolted through me.

"DONNY!" Ryan roared.

My skin glowed gold.

My bones buzzed with raw energy.

And still, I reached.

Until my hand closed around something hard and cold.

With a cry, I pulled my fist free.

The stone circle exploded outward, harmless sparks flying.

My arm trembled, black ash fluttering down.

Evie and Bella were at my side, steadying me as I opened my hand.

Inside?

A corroded metal ring.

The anchor.

The spell.

The lie.

Grandpa Al lifted his face, no longer howling, no longer fading.

He stared at me with something like awe.

"You did it," he whispered.

And for once, the Chicky twins were speechless.

I exhaled, clutching the ring, surrounded by my Trifecta, my Shifter, and my gloriously deranged familiar.

"Let's go home," I said, uttering the first thing that popped into my mind.

But destiny wasn't through with me yet.

EPILOGUE ONE-DONNY

WE WERE STILL behind the Castorini Mausoleum, and Ryan was helping me to my feet slowly.

Time had been moving slowly since the moment my hand closed around the object inside that cursed circle.

I was still processing just how awful the Chicky twins really were and how they got their terrible magic to work.

Hair clippings. Toenail bits. Ash.

All of it reeked of old magic and bad decisions.

These weren't just any clippings either.

They pulsed with remnants of a spell that was as vile as it was petty.

I stood up slowly, my hand trembling, and turned

to glare at the two old Witches trying to do a slow shuffle-scoot toward the tree line.

"Oh, hell no."

I spun on my heel.

"Freeze!"

As if synchronized with my fury, Gryn whipped his hands forward.

A crackling bolt of blue light zipped through the air and locked the Chickazola sisters mid-waddle.

They froze like a pair of dollar-store Halloween decorations, wide-eyed and wrinkled, still dressed like rotting pumpkins in their matching orange sacks.

Ryan stepped closer, eyes scanning the spell remnants still glowing in my palm.

"What is it, Honey?"

I blew out a breath, angry, sad, and grossed out all at once.

"These are magical remnants—hair and nail clippings that should've been burned in the crematorium these two used to own. Standard practice to prevent magical contamination. But instead," I held up the ashes. "They used them to bind Grandpa Al's spirit. Like emotional blackmail with a side of necromancy."

"I told you this was a bad idea," Candice whined.

Only her voice sounded strained since her lips stayed frozen mid-sneer.

"Shut up, Candy!" Denice barked back, her frozen vocal cords vibrating with fury.

It sounded like two trash pandas growling inside a dryer.

I arched a brow. "Charming. Real Witches of the year over here."

Jaxson stepped forward, cracking his knuckles like a bouncer at a magical nightclub.

"Don't worry, I got this," he said, raising a hand.

His voice dropped an octave, thick with magical authority.

"You have the right to remain frozen until such a time as the Morrigan sees fit to throw your heinous, dusty, revenge-obsessed asses into magical lockup for—*let's see*—improper spellcasting, grave-binding, vengeance rituals, and salon libel."

"You tell 'em, baby!" Evie fist-pumped beside him.

I would've laughed if my ghostly grandfather hadn't been visibly flickering, looking like someone was fast-forwarding his soul into oblivion.

"Shit," I whispered, then blinked up at the sky.

Nothing. No lightning. Huh.

Maybe the Goddess knew I kinda deserved a wee break.

I dropped to my knees and whispered a counter-spell over the hateful little circle the twins had used to keep Grandpa Al trapped.

The rocks shimmered and melted into hay, and I dumped the clippings on top.

Bella and Evie were already at my side, linking hands with mine without a word.

"This part, we do together," I said.

We closed our eyes and summoned the power that bound us—the Trifecta of Castor's Corner.

Our magic twined together like the braids our mothers once wove in our hair, and flames rose from our circle in a clean, bright gold.

Then, with a mighty rumble of thunder, a splash of pink, aqua, and gold glitter sparkles, the curse broke with a resounding pop.

Grandpa Al's form solidified in front of us—*still missing the family jewels, but finally, blessedly whole in spirit.*

"Grazie, ragazzi," he whispered with a soft, rakish grin. "Molto bene. Ciao ciao, bambini belli!"

With a wave and a wink, he blew us kisses and faded into a soft, silvery light.

Gone at last, to the Next Amazing Journey.

"We did it!"

"Oh, Donny, you were great!"

Evie and Bella embraced me, and for the first time in a while, I felt good. Really good.

Later that night.

After an hour of magical Swoosh calls—mainly with Magdelena or La Befana—all confirming the Chicky twins were getting their one-way trip to Magical Time-Out, I finally made it to bed.

And as soon as we got through the bedroom door, I melted into Ryan's kiss.

"You did good today, Honey," he growled against my lips.

"You think so?"

"I know so. I'm so proud of you, Donatella."

"Yeah? How about you show me?"

"I can do that," he grumbled, and with a wiggle and a wave, I had us both undressed in record time.

The man was so good at this. At making me forget everything but him.

Like he was the only thing in the whole universe, and he was made just to make me feel good.

"That's not far from the truth, Honey."

Then he was between my legs, licking at my slick sex and making that familiar hum buzz inside my blood and heat build from my core.

Pleasure threatened to catapult me into outer space, but my Bear had me. I knew he did.

He was my anchor. My reason. My protector and my cheerleader.

Goddess, I loved him so.

My fingers threaded in his hair as the first spirals of pleasure began to undo me, and before I finished crying out his name, he was filling me with his thick, curved, perfectly long cock.

"Heaven. You feel like heaven, Donatella."

"You feel like mine, Ryan. I never want to be without you."

"I am yours. You won't ever be without me, mate. Mine," he growled.

Then he pumped his hips, and I wrapped my legs tight around his waist, and together, we exploded like a supernova. His teeth found my mating mark, and he bit me again, claiming me like I hoped he would do again and again, a hundred thousand times or more before we were through with this world.

"I love you, Honey."

"I love you, too."

That night, wrapped up in a tangle of limbs and sweat-slicked skin, I felt safe again.

Anchored.

His fingers traced lazy circles over my hip while his nose nuzzled into the crook of my neck, right where my mating mark glowed faintly.

"Donny?" he murmured.

"Yeah?" I whispered back, half-asleep, fully content.

He pulled something out from under his pillow—*a velvet blue box*—and my heart leapt into my throat.

"It's a little late, but happy birthday."

I sat up, clutching the sheet to my chest. "Is that what I think it is?"

"It could be earrings," he said, all innocence and smirk.

"And you could be sleeping alone for a week," I shot back.

He barked out a laugh and flipped the lid open.

Inside sat a massive, glittering, princess-cut yellow diamond, bright as my magic and as warm as honey.

"Will you marry me, my Witch with the honey hair?"

Tears spilled before I could even speak.

I wiped them away with the sheet and sniffled, grinning like an idiot.

"So, you like the blonde now?"

He growled low and reverently.

"Honey, I flove it."

And then he spent the next few hours proving just how much.

Over. And over. Again.

Grrrrr.

Ryan's head popped up, a lopsided grin on his handsome face.

"You hungry, Honey?"

"For you? Always, Smokey," I said and crashed my lips to his.

I knew things were never going to be easy in Castor's Corner.

Trouble here was like the tide—steady, inevitable, and often full of teeth.

The kind of place where spells backfired, Ghosts held grudges, and magical creatures showed up with baggage, drama, and a flair for the ridiculous.

But for the first time in my life, I wasn't afraid of what might come next.

Because I wasn't going to face it alone.

I had my girls. My cousins. My magical ride-or-dies.

Our Trifecta was stronger than ever—three Witches bonded not just by blood, but by love, loyalty, and a whole lot of magical mischief.

We'd stared down curses, chaos, and the Ghosts of boyfriends past—*and come out glittering on the other side.*

I had Gryn. My grumpy little Domovyk familiar

who used to curse me with blonde streaks and launch me out of bed when I wallowed too long.

Okay, sure—he'd tried to kill me a few times.

But in his defense, he was underfed and underloved.

Now that he was getting his tributes, he'd mellowed into something halfway decent.

Almost charming. In a goblin-esque, homicidally loyal kind of way.

And I had Ryan.

My Bear.

My sweet, strong, sexy-as-hell, croissant-baking mate.

The man who saw every messy, magical, vulnerable part of me and loved me more because of it.

He didn't just stand by me—he chose me. Every day.

With his big hands and bigger heart.

With his soft grumbles and hard muscles.

With those warm, velvet eyes that said *you're mine* in every glance.

And I was.

I was his.

And he was mine.

I didn't know what was coming next. In Castor's Corner, anything was possible.

Raging storms, ancient curses, haunted appliances.

But no matter what came, I'd meet it head-on.

With glam. With grit. With magic in my veins and my bear at my back.

Because this time around?

This Witch finally knew her worth.

And she wasn't afraid to shine.

The end…for now.

ALSO BY C.D. GORRI

<u>Paranormal Romance Books by Series</u>

A Howlin' Good Fairytale Retelling

Barvale Holiday Tales

Dire Wolf Mates

Hearts of Stone Series

Hungry Fur Love

Island Stripe Pride

Jersey Sure Shifters/EveL Worlds

Lords of Nightfall

Macconwood Pack Novel Series

Macconwood Pack Tales Series

Mated in Hope Falls

Moongate Island Tales

Motley Crewd Shifters

NYC Shifter Tales

Purely Paranormal Romance Books

Speed Dating with the Denizens of the Underworld

The Barvale Clan Tales

The Bear Claw Tales

The Falk Clan Tales

The Guardians of Chaos

The Maverick Pride Tales

The Wardens of Terra

Twice Mated Tales

When Worlds Collide

Witch Shifter Clan

Wyvern Protection Unit

Young Adult/Urban Fantasy Books by Series

Blackthorn Academy For Supernaturals

G'Witches Magical Mysteries Series
Co-written with P. Mattern

The Angela Tanner Files

The Grazi Kelly Novel Series

Witches of Westwood Academy
with Gina Kincade

Contemporary Romance Books by Series & Title

Carolina Rugby Romance

A Reason To Try

The Break Down

A Game of Ruck

Dump Tackle My Heart

Support Your Local Hooker

Sin Bin for the Billionaire

Cherry On Top Tales

Her Yule His Log

His Carrot Her Muffin

Her Chocolate His Bar

His Pickle Her Jam

Her Trick His Treat

His Wood Her Fire

Her Birthday His Package

Jersey Bad Boys

Merciful Lies

Devious Lies

Pitiful Lies

Mergers & Acquisitions

Desperate Measures

Desperate Needs

Desperate Desires

Desperate Actions

Desperate People

Desperate Crimes

Desperate Games

Desperate Secrets

Wild Billionaire Romance

His Wild Obsession

His Wild Temptation

His Wild Seduction

His Wild Attraction

Bonus Scene His Wild Halloween Night

Wrecked Rockstar Romance

Dirty Lyrics

Broken Chords

Wicked Beats

Be sure to check out my BUY DIRECT BUNDLES and get 30% off when you buy available only my website.

Click here for The Official C.D. Gorri Reading List - free download

ABOUT THE AUTHOR

USA Today Bestselling Author C.D. Gorri writes steamy Paranormal & Contemporary Romance and Urban Fantasy packed with heart, humor, and heat.

Join her mailing list here: https://www.cdgorri.com/newsletter

A lifelong book lover, she's rarely without a story in hand, and her own tales reflect that passion. Based in her beloved New Jersey, C.D. weaves the Garden State into many of her stories, grounding even the wildest supernatural adventures with a touch of home.

Her books are fast-paced, full of feels, and always end with a satisfying HEA. You'll meet sassy, curvy heroines and the possessive, love-driven heroes who adore them, whether they're Shifters, Vampires,

Witches, or just morally gray men falling hard in her contemporary worlds.

If you're into fated mates, fierce love, and action-packed romance where loyalty wins and love always triumphs then *welcome*. You're in the right place.

Thanks for reading!

Del mare alla stella,
    C.D. Gorri
    Curvy Heroines & Epic Heroes for the avid reader.
    http://www.cdgorri.com
    https://www.facebook.com/Cdgorribooks
    https://www.bookbub.com/authors/c-d-gorri
    https://twitter.com/cgor22
    https://instagram.com/cdgorri/
    https://www.goodreads.com/cdgorri
    https://www.tiktok.com/@cdgorriauthor